P9-AQO-650

Harlem
NEW YORK

Harris Farm
ELBERFELD,
INDIANA

Shady Acres
Campground
CLAYSVILLE,
PENNSYLVANIA

St. Louis
MISSOURI

Rocking Horse
Ranch
OHIO

Gopher and Gazelle
Campground
WYANDOTTE, OKLAHOMA

N
W    E
S

# THE VANDERBEEKERS
## ON the ROAD

Also by Karina Yan Glaser

*The Vanderbeekers of 141st Street*
*The Vanderbeekers and the Hidden Garden*
*The Vanderbeekers to the Rescue*
*The Vanderbeekers Lost and Found*
*The Vanderbeekers Make a Wish*

*A Duet for Home*

# THE VANDERBEEKERS
## ON the ROAD

By Karina Yan Glaser

CLARION BOOKS
*An Imprint of* HarperCollins*Publishers*

Clarion Books is an imprint of HarperCollins Publishers.

The Vanderbeekers on the Road
Text and illustrations copyright © 2022 by Karina Yan Glaser
Map © 2022 by Jennifer Thermes

ISBN 978-0-35-843457-3

The text is set in Stempel Garamond LT Std.
22 23 24 25 26  LBC  6 5 4 3 2

First Edition

To my favorite road trippers: Lina, Kaela, Dan, Ginger Pye, and Lalo. I love discovering new places with you.

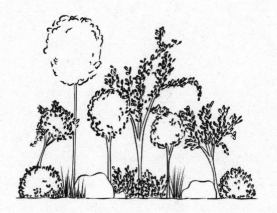

Isn't it splendid to think of all the
things there are to find out about?
It just makes me feel glad to be
alive—it's such an interesting world.

—L.M. Montgomery,
Anne of Green Gables

# Friday, August 8

Miles to California: 3,041

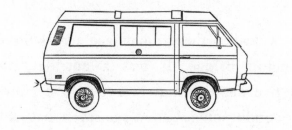

# One

If you had asked the Vanderbeekers whether they ever imagined they would be in a white van with a license plate that said LUDWIG, heading toward Indiana, they would have said it would be more likely that they were going to the moon. But after the events of the past week—having found out that their dad was stuck in Elberfeld, Indiana, after a tornado hit the area and his flight home got canceled and he would miss the big fortieth surprise birthday plans they had for him—the Vanderbeekers took action. And that action required borrowing a van from their friend Mr. Ritchie and convincing Mama that a monthlong road trip was *exactly* what they all needed.

It was 4:32 in the afternoon, the sun still bright

in the sky, when the van chugged across the George Washington Bridge. It was a hot day, close to ninety-five degrees, and everyone was grateful for the air-conditioning. Laney, age seven, had unlatched Tuxedo's carrier and brought the cat onto her lap, and they were staring out the window, watching the familiar New York City skyline get smaller and smaller. The sky spread over the metropolis, and suddenly the big city didn't look so big anymore. Below, the waters of the Hudson River, which separated New York City from New Jersey, rolled in rhythmic waves around the island of Manhattan. And while Laney could not wait to see Papa, her nerves bubbled up as they got farther away from their beloved brownstone. She had never left home for more than a couple of weeks, and this trip was going to be a whole month long.

Laney blinked, and suddenly the city disappeared from view as the van exited the bridge and veered onto a highway.

"Benny cannot believe we're driving across the country," Isa, age fifteen, announced as she checked her phone. Benny was one of Isa's best friends, and his family operated Castleman's Bakery, home of the best cheese croissants in the world. "He says he's going to miss me."

"Of course he's going to miss you," Jessie, Isa's twin sister, said.

"I can't believe we're doing this either," Mama added from the driver's seat.

"Me either," said Mr. Beiderman, their third-floor neighbor. He was in the front passenger seat, a pile of maps on his lap.

Orlando, who was the same age as the twins, spoke up from the back of the van. Mr. B had become his guardian after his mom disappeared and returned to

Georgia without him a year ago. "Mr. B, you don't need those paper maps. I have everything on my phone."

Mr. B tried to straighten the folds of a huge map of New Jersey, causing the paper to rip. "What if we don't have reception? What if the internet is wrong?"

Jessie sat in the back row with Orlando. They glanced at each other and shrugged.

Mr. B and Orlando had only decided to join their trip two hours ago. This was a momentous milestone for Mr. B, who rarely made a hasty decision. Mr. B liked the predictable, which explained the clothes he wore every day. The only times the Vanderbeekers had seen him wearing something other than black pants and a black shirt was during the marathon a year ago, when Laney had made him a sparkly, bejeweled purple T-shirt to run in.

The week had been eventful. The Vanderbeekers had found an old letter that their father's dad, who they all called Pop-Pop, had planned to give to him the day of his college graduation. The letter had laid out plans for a road trip to California complete with stops at landmarks and national parks that Pop-Pop had always wanted to see. But Pop-Pop had died of a heart attack before the graduation, and Papa had never gotten the letter. He never knew about the trip his dad wanted to take with him across the country to Whalers Cove. After much investigation, the Vanderbeekers had put together the pieces of the trip and were now going to surprise Papa by recreating it as a fortieth birthday present.

They had found Pop-Pop's itinerary in Mr. Ritchie's van, and it included four additional places that Pop-Pop had wanted to see during the road trip: St. Louis, Carlsbad Caverns, White Sands National Park, and the Grand Canyon. And, of course, there was Whalers Cove, the final destination, which was in Point Lobos, right by where their Aunt Penny lived in California.

Oliver, age twelve, sat right behind Mr. B and straightened his legs so his feet were flat against the back of Mr. B's seat.

"I can feel that in my lumbar spine," Mr. B said.

"There's nowhere else for me to put my feet!" Oliver said. "We're transporting a whole zoo with us!"

Oliver was not wrong. There was Tuxedo, of course, and their basset hound, Franz, and then Mama and Laney had made an unscheduled stop at the Treehouse

Bakery and Cat Café, the store that Mama owned, to pick up Peaches and Cream, two bonded sister cats. They were bringing the cats to California for Aunt Penny. Because the crate had to hold two cats as well as a litter box, it was quite large, and there was nowhere for it to go but on the floor in front of Oliver's seat.

Tuxedo jumped off Laney's shoulder and onto the floor, peering through the crate bars at the unexpected guests. Peaches or Cream—Oliver could not tell them apart—hissed and stuck a paw out to swipe at him. Tuxedo recoiled, his tail immediately puffing out as if he'd been electrocuted.

"Great," Oliver grumbled. "The cats are fighting."

"They're just getting to know each other," Laney said as Tuxedo leapt into her lap.

"Why is Tuxedo out of his carrier?" Mama asked as the van slowed to a crawl. It was rush hour, and it seemed as if the whole state of New Jersey was on this particular highway.

"He doesn't like it in there," Laney reported. "He wants freedom."

Hyacinth, age nine and the quietest of the Vanderbeeker siblings, was sitting in the first row with Franz, next to Oliver. Franz, not a fan of cars, was drooling. Oliver kept moving farther away from him so as not to get wet.

"It's okay, Franz," Hyacinth whispered, wiping his chin with a handkerchief she had embroidered with lilacs. "We're going to California!"

Franz whimpered, then collapsed into her lap and let Hyacinth rub behind his ears.

"Can you send her another text?" Mama was saying to Mr. Beiderman, who had her phone in his hands and was madly typing. "I don't want Auntie Harrigan to forget that flour order."

Auntie Harrigan was Mama's sister-in-law, married to Mama's brother, Arthur, and she had agreed to take over the bakery for the month. A ping sounded.

"Harrigan says she knows and to stop bothering her and concentrate on the road," Mr. B reported before switching her phone ringer off. "And now this is going in the glove compartment."

Isa put in her earbuds to listen to music, while Hyacinth hunched over her notebook. Oliver immersed himself in a copy of *Rez Dogs*.

"Holy smokes," Orlando said in a quiet voice. "Did

you see this email?"

Curious, Laney listened in on the conversation behind her.

"Wow," Jessie said. "Do you think we should do it?"

"But it's your dad's birthday trip," Orlando said. "We shouldn't be doing school stuff during vacation, right?"

"It's a once-in-a-lifetime opportunity!" Jessie said. "I think we should tell her yes."

Laney couldn't take the suspense anymore. She turned around. "What once-in-a-lifetime opportunity?" she asked.

Jessie and Orlando looked at her, then at each other. Then they did that thing where they talked with their eyes, before Jessie turned back to Laney.

"It's nothing," Jessie said. "Just something for school."

They returned to their phones, and Laney could tell they were texting each other. Knowing she wouldn't get more information from them, Laney turned back around. She was going to figure out what they were up to—it was just a matter of finding the right opportunity.

Mama tapped the steering wheel. "I cannot believe we're driving across the country!"

"Papa is going to be *so* surprised," Laney said, and Tuxedo meowed in agreement.

"I'm hungry," Oliver announced.

"We've only been on the road for forty-one minutes," Jessie told him.

"Are we almost there?" Laney asked.

"Sure," Jessie said. "Just twelve hours left until we get to Elberfeld."

"*Twelve hours?*" Laney yelped.

"It might be longer," Mama said, "depending on traffic. Friday-night traffic is the worst."

Laney sighed and glanced out the window. There were *so* many cars.

"We're going all the way to Indiana," Isa told her. "We have to go through New Jersey, Pennsylvania, Ohio, and Kentucky."

"And after we pick up Papa," Jessie added, "it will be another really long drive until we get to California. We're going all the way across America."

"Here, I'll show you a map," Mr. Beiderman said, shuffling through his paper maps. Then his phone rang. He glanced at the caller ID, then turned his ringer off.

"Who was that?" Laney asked.

"It's a work thing," Mr. B said. Mr. B was a professor of art history at City College.

"Someone is calling on a Friday night?" Mama asked.

Mr. B sighed. "They're reorganizing our department and hired a new director. This new person keeps calling and scheduling meetings. I need to let him know I'll be out of touch this month."

"He sounds terrible," Laney said. "What's his name?"

"Dennis," Mr. B said. "Dennis Stone."

"Are you sure it's okay for us to be gone all month?" Orlando asked from the back of the van. "I don't want you to get in trouble with your new boss."

"It's fine," Mr. B said. "Most faculty take August off. And I plan on working from the road."

As Mr. B typed an email to his new boss on his phone, Laney moved Tuxedo's crate so it was right under her feet and could serve as a footstool. She grabbed her backpack and opened it. Inside was her favorite blanket, as well as seven stuffed animals, eight books, two erasers, four pieces of candy, a stubby pencil, and a pack of markers that was missing the yellow one. She removed a book, only to have it snatched out of her hands by Oliver.

"Laney was going to read a book!" Oliver reported, holding it aloft.

"Laney! You know better than that!" Jessie scolded.

"What?" Laney said. "Oliver is reading a book!"

"Reading makes you carsick," Isa reminded her.

"You have your barf bucket, right?" Mama asked.

"Yep!" Laney picked up the bucket, a gallon bin that had previously held caramel popcorn.

"No reading in the car," Oliver said, tossing the book next to him. It landed on Franz, who startled, then shook himself, spraying dog slobber everywhere.

"We need to deep-clean this van before returning it to Mr. Ritchie," Mr. B murmured to Mama.

"Or buy him a brand-new one," Mama agreed.

"I have nothing to do if I can't read!" Laney protested.

"Just sit there without moving," Oliver advised. "Do whatever you need to do to keep from throwing up."

Laney frowned and looked out the window. There wasn't much to look at. Big stores, and so many cars. They passed a driver who looked as if she was singing to a song on the radio, then a driver who was picking something out of his teeth, then a driver picking his *nose,* then a driver applying lipstick while waiting for traffic to ease up.

"Jessie," Mama said. "Any luck finding us somewhere to stay tonight?"

Jessie, who had been using her phone to look up lodging, shook her head. "Everything is so expensive!"

"It's August," Mr. Beiderman said. "Everyone is traveling for summer vacation."

"The cheapest room I can find along our route in Pennsylvania is a hundred and seventy dollars per night for four people," she said. "And that's without taxes or the twenty-dollar pet fee per animal."

"Yikes," said Isa, who was in charge of the Fiver Account, a savings fund they had all been contributing to for the last year. Mr. Beiderman had added to it that afternoon, working it out with Mama that he would put in one-third of what the Vanderbeekers had already saved. "How are we going to get all the way across the country and back if that's how much hotels cost?"

"I can help research places to stay," Oliver offered. "Wait, I don't have a phone." He glared at Mama.

"I can feel you glaring at me, Oliver," Mama said.

"This one is a little cheaper," Jessie said. "It's a hundred and fifty dollars. Oops, they don't take pets. Too bad this van isn't a trailer. There are plenty of places to park a trailer."

"We can camp," Oliver suggested. "We have all the camping stuff with us."

Oliver was supposed to have gone camping with Papa as a special summer-after-sixth-grade trip, but it had been canceled when Papa had had to go to Indiana unexpectedly. They had been collecting borrowed camping supplies for the past month, and Oliver had insisted on loading it all into the van for the road trip.

"I thought you brought that in case you and Papa could get away to camp for a few days in California," Mama said.

"I did," Oliver said, "but we've got two tents. Each one holds four people. Jimmy L let me borrow both."

"I'll look up campsites," Jessie said, and she went back to her phone.

"I don't like sleeping outside," Mr. Beiderman announced.

"Neither do I," Isa said.

"C'mon," Oliver said. "The fresh air! The stars! The quiet!"

"The bears!" Isa said.

"The poison ivy!" Mr. Beiderman added.

"The mosquitoes!" Laney chimed in.

"We have to make the Fiver Account last," Jessie said, swiping away at her phone. "And campsites *are* much cheaper. This one only costs twenty dollars!"

"Wow, really?" Mama said.

"It's right next to a lake, too!" Jessie said.

"Book it," Oliver ordered.

# Two

It was dark by the time Ludwig Van rolled into Shady Acres Campground. The site was off I-76, not far from Pittsburgh. The five-and-a-half-hour drive had extended to nearly eight hours due to traffic, a stop for pizza, and a couple of bathroom breaks. Everyone except Laney and Orlando was cranky.

"Yikes!" Oliver said as he peered out the window into the darkness. A derelict sign missing some letters hung from a post.

"We should have paid for the hotel rooms," Jessie murmured to Orlando.

Mr. Beiderman, who had taken over driving after dinner, pulled into a tiny parking area in front of a minuscule cabin with rows of dolls sitting in the windows. The cabin was illuminated from the inside, giving the dolls a creepy I'm-watching-you look. Above the front door was a faded sign that said CHECK IN HERE.

"I don't want to go in there," Hyacinth said as she

stared at the cabin. "This place gives me the creeps."

"I'll check in," Mama said. "Jessie, come with me since you made the reservation."

Jessie reluctantly unbuckled her seat belt, squeezed past the others, and hopped out of the van.

"I'll call for help if you're not back in five," Oliver promised.

Jessie rolled her eyes, and Oliver watched as they knocked on the cabin door. A moment later, the door opened and Oliver could see an older woman with hair in two long braids wearing full rain gear: a bright yellow raincoat, a wide-brimmed hat, and galoshes.

"Why is she dressed like that?" Laney asked.

"The weather was clear when we stopped for dinner," Isa said. She checked the weather app on her phone. "Says it's going to be clear all night."

Oliver craned his neck to look at the sky through the window, but it was dark and they were surrounded by too many trees. At his feet, Peaches and Cream were restless in their carrier.

"Do we have any cat food?" Oliver asked.

"I think I saw it back here," Orlando said, leaning over the back seat of the last row in the van, moving luggage and camping equipment aside to unearth a shopping bag. "Here it is!"

They passed the bin of cat food up to Oliver, and he opened the gate. Peaches and Cream, terrified about their abrupt change of situation, huddled in the back of the carrier, their green eyes glowing in the darkness. Oliver poured kibble into the food bowl, accidentally spilling some on the floor of the van, and Tuxedo promptly gulped it up. Oliver closed the gate.

"What's taking so long?" Laney said, restless. "I'm tired of sitting."

"I think that doll just moved," Isa said, staring at the cabin windows.

The cabin door opened, and Oliver breathed a sigh of relief to see Mama and Jessie appear.

Mama opened the passenger-side door and slid back into the seat, handing a sheet of paper to Mr. Beiderman. "Directions to our campsite. We're number eighteen, next to the lake."

The sliding door opened, and Jessie got in. She was carrying a cord of wood. "Well, that was weird."

"What happened?" Laney asked.

"First of all, Sally the camp owner said not to worry

about the bears," Jessie said.

"Bears?" Isa squeaked.

"Oh, heck no," Mr. B said, and he slowly drove along the rocky path. "Bears? I'm sleeping in the van tonight."

"We *don't* need to worry about the bears," Jessie repeated. "What we have to watch out for is Rocco."

"Who's Rocco?" asked Oliver, Isa, Laney, Hyacinth, Orlando, and Mr. B.

"Apparently a very wily raccoon," Jessie said.

"Honestly, I'm still more worried about the bears," Isa said. "How many are there?"

"She didn't say," Jessie said.

Mr. Beiderman was squinting out the window, looking for number eighteen. "I think we missed it," he said as they passed a sign that said 21. The path was so narrow that he had to make a five-point turn to go in the other direction.

"I think it's that path," Mama said, pointing.

Mr. B stopped the van, and Mama jumped out and looked around. She turned and gave a thumbs-up. The van pulled in while Mama picked up the sign marker for number 18, which looked as if it had been run over and then chewed on by a large wild animal.

Mr. B parked, and everyone hopped out of the van into the warm summer night. Franz immediately began sniffing everything. Orlando grabbed the camping lantern under his seat and turned it on.

Oliver had never seen a more depressing campsite. There was a wooden picnic table with a wide slat missing from the top. The benches looked full of splinters. Next to the table was a circle of rocks around a mountain of ash from previous campfires.

"Where's the lake?" Laney asked.

"According to the map," Mama said, "it's that way."

They took the lantern with them down a short path, where there was a small puddle of water, about the size of the toddler swimming pool Laney had used when she was two.

"That's just sad," Orlando said, shaking his head.

"It's a breeding ground for mosquitoes!" Jessie said, quickly turning around and heading back to the campsite, swatting at her neck.

Mr. Beiderman, also not a fan of mosquitoes, followed Jessie to the van and released the bungee cords that secured the tents and Laney's bike to the roof rack. Orlando and Oliver helped him take the tents down.

"Who knows how to set up a tent?" Mama said.

"Don't look at me," Mr. Beiderman said.

"I've never been camping," Orlando added.

"Papa usually puts up the tent," Laney said.

"I think I remember how to do it," Oliver said. "First you have to choose the place where you want the tent."

"Is anyone else getting bitten by mosquitoes?" Jessie asked.

"Then we slide the camp stuff out of the bag," Oliver said as he upended the bag so the contents spilled out onto the dirt, "and unfold the tent, and then do something with these stakes."

"I don't think that's specific enough," Isa said, sifting through the items. "Aren't there directions or something?"

"I'm looking it up online," Jessie said, pulling out her phone. "And . . . there's no internet service."

"Like I said, the internet is unreliable," Mr. Beiderman said. "Aren't you glad I brought paper maps?"

"Not really," Jessie replied, swatting at another

mosquito, "because what we really need is tent directions!"

Laney rubbed her eyes. "Can we sleep yet?"

Mama squinted at her watch. "Goodness, is it already ten o'clock? Yes, Laney, you need to get to bed. Hyacinth, how are you feeling, honey? Why don't I take you both to the bathroom, and maybe by the time we get back the tents will be up." Mama led Laney and Hyacinth back onto the main path, where they had passed bathrooms on the way in. A breeze blew through the campsite, which was well received by everyone.

"I'm pretty sure you just sort of slide those long thingamajigs into the tent sleeves," Oliver said, "and it's supposed to work."

Mr. Beiderman helped him put the tent poles inside the sleeves, but the poles didn't fit together.

"I think the poles have to be connected in sections," Orlando said, looking at them again. "You have to put them together in a specific order."

They took the poles out of the sleeves and started over. The wind picked up. Laney and Hyacinth returned, ready to go to bed, and Mama sighed when she saw all the tent pieces still on the ground.

"Laney, why don't you sleep in the van with Tuxedo tonight," Mama said.

"But I want to sleep in a tent!" Laney said, starting to cry. "Oliver promised!"

"No, I didn't," Oliver snapped as he struggled with the tent poles. "I just *suggested* camping since hotels were so expensive!"

"I'm sure you'll figure the tents out," Mama said to Oliver.

Thankfully, Laney cheered up when Mama said they could open the door to Peaches and Cream's crate for the night so the cats could move around. Hyacinth followed Mama and Laney, hoping no one would notice she wasn't helping with the tent setup. The van was stuffy, so Mama rolled down the windows to let in the breeze. "See?" she said. "It's practically like sleeping outside."

Laney lay down across the first row of seats, while Hyacinth took the second. Franz jumped up and tried to snuggle as close to her as possible, confused by the whole situation. Even though the door to the big crate was open, Peaches and Cream refused to come out.

"They just need to get used to this new experience,"

Mama explained. "It's an adjustment."

Jessie, meanwhile, had been outside examining the poles and had figured out how to put them together while simultaneously slapping the mosquitoes that were landing on her in droves. After the poles were assembled, they could finally slide them through the sleeves of the tent. Unfortunately, before they could drive in the stakes to secure the tent to the ground, a wind whipped through the campsite, upending the tent and causing it to tumble toward the "lake."

"Catch it before it goes in!" Jessie yelled, and everyone raced after it.

It was too late. The tent landed in the lake and immediately got bogged down with water. Orlando dragged it out.

"I bet there are millions of mosquito eggs on that tent now," Jessie said with a shiver.

They brought the tent back to the campsite, shook it dry, then managed to stake it all down before another gust could take it away.

"Success!" Oliver said.

"I can't believe we have to put up another one," Isa said. "I'm exhausted."

But just as Oliver was about to open the bag containing the second tent, there was a crack of thunder, and buckets of rain fell from the sky.

✿ ✿ ✿

Mr. Beiderman, Orlando, Isa, Jessie, and Oliver crawled into the tent they had already put up. The four-person tent was way too small for five people, especially when Orlando was built like a football player and Mr. B was nearly six feet tall.

They realized something else. They were sitting on the bare ground, and water was starting to seep in.

"Wasn't there supposed to be ground cloth or tarp or something?" Jessie asked.

"I don't remember seeing a ground cloth in the tent bag," Orlando said. He peeked out the entrance. "Oh, I see it now. It's all wet."

"Maybe we can use the tarp that Hyacinth has been using to cover the seat to protect it from Franz," Isa said.

"I'll get it," Orlando volunteered, and he crawled out and grabbed the wet tarp, then dragged the second tent under the van so it wouldn't get soaked from the rain. Then he picked up Laney's bicycle, opened the van door, and disappeared inside.

"I don't think he's coming back," Oliver reported.

"I wouldn't if I were him," Isa said.

"Mama is already asleep in the front seat," Oliver said. "Lucky." More water was coming in and the ground squished under his sneakers.

"We can't stay here like this all night," Jessie said.

"Orlando is coming back!" Oliver said, moving to make space for Orlando to crawl back through the opening.

"Sorry, Hyacinth and Franz were already asleep on top of the tarp and it was hard to get it out from under them," Orlando said. "Okay, how do we do this?"

Everyone moved to the edges of the tent so they could lay the tarp down and spread it across the ground.

"Since this tent only accommodates four people," Mr. Beiderman said, "that means one person gets to sleep in the van."

"Me!" said Isa, Jessie, Orlando, and Oliver at once.

After a few heated rounds of rock, paper, scissors, Isa won and gleefully raced for the van.

"Lucky," Oliver grumbled again.

"All right, everyone take their shoes off," Jessie said. They removed their muddy sneakers and piled them in a corner by the entrance, then settled down on the tarp.

"Man, this is super uncomfortable," Orlando said, shifting.

"We were in such a rush to get the tent up," Oliver said, "we didn't check the ground for rocks."

"I'm lying on a hundred rocks right now," Jessie said. "Maybe a thousand."

"I hope bears don't like rain," Orlando said.

"I've never met a bear," Oliver said. "I sort of want to."

"Not me," Jessie said. "I can never remember what to do around wildlife. Sometimes you're supposed to retreat, sometimes you're supposed to yell and make noise, and sometimes you're not supposed to make eye contact."

"With bears, I think you're supposed to run," Oliver said. "No, wait, I think you're supposed to make noise."

"Hopefully we won't see one," Mr. B said, closing his eyes. "Now will you be quiet? I have to drive tomorrow."

Orlando switched off the lantern, and the tent was engulfed in darkness. The sound of rain, which was usually so calming, seemed menacing against the thin walls. Water crept in from a hole next to him, and he felt his T-shirt getting wet. Then he heard a cracking sound outside. Oliver poked his head out the entrance, but it was so dark he couldn't see a thing.

"Oliver, close the flap," Jessie grumbled. "You're letting rain in."

Oliver zipped the entrance closed and lay back down. There were so many rocks under him! He turned to his side, then, finding that even more uncomfortable, rolled onto his back again, only to land in another puddle of rainwater. Mr. B had already fallen asleep and was now snoring, irritating Oliver and making it impossible to drift off.

This was turning out to be the worst road trip ever.

✵ ✵ ✵

Jessie lay in her sleeping bag, staring up at the top of the tent. Mr. Beiderman and Orlando had fallen asleep immediately, but Oliver was awake for at least another hour before his breath evened out and his body relaxed into slumber. Even though she was exhausted, Jessie couldn't find a comfortable spot and yearned for her own bed in the brownstone. She wondered how Grandma and Grandpa were doing back in Harlem, living in the Vanderbeekers' apartment and working at Mama's bakery. It was funny to think about her grandparents there by themselves while the Vanderbeekers were on a three-thousand-mile journey across America.

Jessie sighed and shifted, remembering the email she and Orlando had received that afternoon. It was from their science teacher, Ms. Brown, who had been their adviser for their last few science projects. They were supposed to be working on a new project with her in August in preparation for the New York City Science and Engineering Fair in the fall, but Orlando and Jessie had emailed to let her know that they were heading to California and wouldn't be able to meet in person.

They had expected Ms. Brown to be upset, but

instead they received a very different response. Jessie turned her phone on, dimming the screen so as not to wake everyone, and opened her notes to where she had saved the email.

*Dear Jessie and Orlando,*

*Thank you for letting me know about your change of August plans. This is actually fortuitous because there is a very special opportunity that I wanted to let you know about. The University of California at Berkeley offers a scholarship prize for science, and the application process is overseen by an esteemed professor of astrophysics, Dr. Daniela Bonavita. To be eligible, you need to be on track to complete high school in three years. If you're a finalist, you must interview in person with her. I had originally only been looking at scholarship contests for you on the East Coast, but since you're going to be in California I think you should fill out the application. It would be* a quick turnaround—the application is due this Monday—and if you're a finalist, then the interview day with Dr. Bonavita would be on Wednesday, August 20. Do you think you'll be in California by then?

I strongly encourage you to apply if at all possible. They select two students each year to do a summer science program after sophomore year—travel expenses, room, and board all included—and it leads to a full scholarship to Berkeley upon completion of high school in three years. I think the two of you are perfect candidates for this award. As you know, I myself went to Berkeley and loved it. They have a fantastic science program, and I think you would both thrive there.

I will send the link to the application in a second email. Please do let me know if you have any questions or if you would like to discuss further.

Sincerely,
Ms. Brown

A full scholarship to Berkeley! Jessie couldn't imagine a better opportunity for them. Next to her, Orlando stirred and turned to face her.

"You still awake?" he said quietly, his voice sleepy.

"Yeah," she whispered back. She looked at Oliver and Mr. B, who were both sound asleep, then switched off her phone. Darkness filled the tent. "Just thinking about the email Ms. Brown sent us."

She could hear Orlando sit up, but it was so dark she couldn't see him.

"Do you really think we should apply?" Orlando said. "I mean, what are the odds that we would actually win? I bet there are hundreds of great applicants. And I don't want to take away from the road trip."

"We might not even be finalists," Jessie said. "What's the harm of applying just to see?"

"I guess we can try," Orlando said. "But I don't want Mr. Beiderman or your family to know. You know how they'll get."

"You mean all supportive and excited and constantly asking us how it's going?"

"Exactly. When we aren't finalists, we won't have to explain. They won't be disappointed."

Orlando settled back down into his sleeping bag, and a few minutes later his breathing evened out. Jessie turned onto her side, trying to ignore a rock digging into her ribs. What they hadn't talked about was how a full scholarship to UC Berkeley would change both of their lives. Orlando didn't like talking about money, so Jessie hadn't brought it up.

As Jessie stared into the darkness, she thought about what Orlando had said and wondered if he was afraid of disappointing himself most of all.

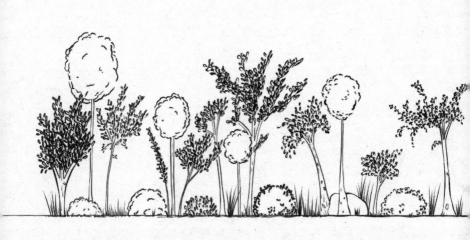

# SATURDAY, AUGUST 9

Miles to Monterey: 2,661

# Three

"Rise and shine!" *Ring, ring!* "Rise and shine!" *Ring, ring!*

Jessie woke to the sound of Laney yelling and relentlessly ringing her bike bell. Oliver's elbow was jabbing into her ribs, while on her other side, Orlando's arm was flung over her face. Mr. Beiderman had rolled into the edge of the tent in his sleep. The air was hot and muggy, a result of keeping the tent closed because of the rain. She peeked at her watch. It was 6:32 a.m.

Jessie blinked, removed Orlando's heavy arm from her face, and pushed Oliver away. She sat up, rolled her neck, and winced. Sleeping on the rocky ground without a pillow was no fun at all. She scratched absently at her arms, then looked closer at the red bumps. She had at least thirty mosquito bites.

"Hey," Orlando said, moving next to her, his voice rough with sleep. "I think I slept a grand total of two hours."

"Me too," Jessie said. "I bet you're already regretting coming on this road trip."

Orlando sat up. "Life is never boring with you all, that's for sure. I've never really gone on a vacation, so this is . . . an experience."

"Really?" Jessie said, turning to him.

"Rise and shine!" yelled Laney. *Ring, ring!* "Rise and shine!" *Ring, ring!*

"I've gone to New York to visit Aunt Josie and Uncle Jeet," Orlando said, "but I've never gone on a vacation with my mom."

"Do you miss her?" Jessie asked.

A year ago, the Vanderbeekers had discovered that Orlando had been living in the community garden's shed. His mom had disappeared, which is why Mr. Beiderman now took care of him.

"I talked to her a week ago," Orlando said. "She's still in Georgia. Mr. Beiderman said he would take me down to visit her for Thanksgiving if I want."

"Will you go?"

"I'm not sure," Orlando said, then changed the subject. "If we're going to camp all the way across the country, I need a mat and a pillow."

"And bug spray," Jessie said, scratching at another mosquito bite. She took out her phone and looked at it. "Still no reception. I don't even know if we can fill out the Berkeley application with the type of cell service we're getting."

"Rise and shine!" *Ring, ring!* "Rise and shine!" *Ring, ring!* It sounded as if Laney was now circling their tent.

Jessie rolled her eyes and leaned over to open the tent flap. "We hear you!"

Laney's bike squealed to a stop by the tent, and Laney leaned down to look at them. "What were you talking about?" she said.

"Nothing," Jessie and Orlando said in unison.

Laney narrowed her eyes. "I thought I heard you saying something about an application. What's it for?"

Jessie and Orlando exchanged a look; then Jessie said, "We were just talking about what we're going to do today."

"Really?"

"Really."

Laney pursed her lips. "Mama says we need to get on the road as soon as possible. She says she needs coffee."

"Mrmphhhh," Oliver said as he started to wake up next to Jessie.

"Remind me never to road-trip with you again," Mr. Beiderman mumbled. He still made no move to get up.

"Get up!" Laney said. "Did you see any bears? Oliver, why are you all wet?"

Jessie looked over at Oliver. He and Mr. Beiderman had gotten the worst sleeping spots, right against each edge of the tent, where the rain came in. Oliver had taken the brunt of it, and when he sat up, Jessie saw that his clothes were all wet and muddy.

Oliver looked really grumpy, so Jessie thought it best to exit the tent and get ready to leave. She looked at the corner where they had left their shoes the night before, but they weren't there. She crawled out of the tent and looked around, but their shoes were nowhere to be found.

"Uh, we have a problem," Jessie said at the same time Orlando asked, "Where are our shoes?"

❋ ❋ ❋

Hyacinth left the camp bathroom, grateful not to have to go in there ever again. The structure was crumbling and had at least a thousand spiders in it. She shivered. Spiders were the reason she was glad she lived in a city and not the country. Even the thought of having a whole farm full of animals wasn't enough to make her want to move. Franz trotted next to her, happy to be out of the van.

They returned to the campsite to find Mama trying to coax Peaches and Cream to eat. Mr. Beiderman, Orlando, Oliver, and Jessie were standing outside the tent, all barefoot. Their feet sank into the muddy ground. They looked disheveled and exhausted.

"Their shoes disappeared!" Laney reported when she saw Hyacinth. "A bear must have taken them!"

"I think bears are more interested in food, not shoes," Isa said, coming out of the van. Her hair was brushed and she was wearing a floral tank top and cutoff jean shorts. Then she caught sight of the tent sleepers. "Whoa, what happened to you?"

"We slept in a tent during a rainstorm, what do you think?" Oliver snapped.

"Yikes, sorry," Isa said.

"Where could our shoes be?" Jessie wondered.

A man walking down the main campground path overheard their conversation and stopped. He was wearing a fishing vest, long pants, and waders. A fishing pole was over one shoulder, and he held a tackle box in his other hand. "Did your shoes get stolen?"

The Vanderbeekers, Mr. B, and Orlando nodded.

"Rocco strikes again," the man said with the wisdom of someone who was well acquainted with Rocco.

"The *raccoon?*" Oliver said.

"Yep," the man said. "He got my sneakers when I was here a few weeks ago."

"Does he have a den where he might have taken them?" Mr. Beiderman asked. "Those were my favorite running shoes."

"I don't think you're going to want your shoes back after he's taken them," the man said. "But if you want to look for them, you should go that way." He pointed in the direction of the "lake."

They headed that way, Jessie, Oliver, Mr. Beiderman, and Orlando walking tentatively down the path, wincing as the rocks dug into their bare feet.

"I see them!" Laney exclaimed, pointing.

Right in the middle of the puddle-lake were their shoes, submerged in the muddy water.

"You've got to be kidding," Mr. Beiderman said.

"That's one twisted raccoon," Oliver said.

"If he was able to get our shoes, that means he was in our tent," Jessie said with a shudder. "I need a shower, pronto."

"That's the one pair of shoes I brought with me," Orlando said.

"Me too," Mr. Beiderman, Jessie, and Oliver said.

"You can borrow mine," Isa said to Jessie. "I brought two pairs of sneakers."

"That's what we get for packing light," Oliver said.

They walked back to the campsite to find Mama trying to take the tent down.

"We've got to get moving," Mama said, yanking the muddy stakes out of the ground. "I don't know about you, Mr. B, but I need coffee as soon as possible.

We've got a long drive ahead of us—what happened to your shoes?"

"Rocco," everyone replied.

"Stole them and sunk them in the lake," Jessie explained.

Mama closed her eyes and took a deep, calming breath. When she opened her eyes again, she said, "We'll stop by a store on our way to Indiana. Help me take this tent down."

Isa made Laney run laps around the campsite to get out some of her energy while everyone else packed up. Mr. B took down the tents and put them back on top of the van with Laney's bike. Then the four barefoot campers wiped their feet, climbed into the van, and buckled up. Franz commenced his anxious drooling. Isa took a seat with Jessie in the back, Orlando bravely sat next to Hyacinth and Franz in the middle row, and Oliver and Laney took the spots they had had the day before. Oliver grumbled about having to sit with Peaches and Cream again, although Hyacinth guessed that he actually was quite fond of the cats, as he'd been the first one in the van and had had first pick of seats. Laney took a book out of her backpack, which was snatched away immediately, and Mama adjusted the driver's seat and mirrors. Mr. Beiderman organized his maps.

"Everyone buckled up?" Mama asked.

There was a chorus of affirmatives, and Mama started Ludwig Van and they crunched down the rocky path. In daylight, the campground was even shabbier than it had appeared the night before. They passed by the main check-in cabin, where Sally the camp owner was standing in the doorway. She was wearing shorts and a T-shirt and waved as they passed.

"Guess there won't be rain today," Jessie said, observing her outfit.

"Good riddance, Sady Cres Capround," Oliver said as they rolled by the dilapidated sign.

Mama turned the van back onto I-76, heading toward Indiana.

"GPS says eight hours and thirty-two minutes until we reach Elberfeld," Jessie announced from the back of the van.

"Papa, here we come!" Laney said.

# Four

Isa shifted in her seat. They had been in the van for two hours. Next to her, Jessie had fallen asleep, toppled over in exhaustion so her head was resting in Isa's lap. While Isa felt sorry for everyone who had slept in the tent last night, she sure was glad she'd slept in the van. Even from the safety of the vehicle, the rain had been incredibly loud, and she couldn't imagine sleeping in a tent with flimsy walls in the middle of such a ferocious rainstorm. The only bad thing was that Laney was a sleep talker. Hyacinth, used to this behavior because she and Laney shared a room, managed to murmur comforting words without fully waking up herself. Isa, on the other hand, woke up startled, thinking that Laney really did need to go to Coney Island that very minute or replace her bike because Tuxedo had eaten it.

Because the previous day had been so hectic, Isa hadn't had time to practice her violin. It ruined her streak of practicing every day. The last time she'd missed a day of practice had been a year ago, when they were helping Uncle Arthur with a project for Habitat for Humanity and they ended up staying at the construction site from early morning until midnight.

Looking at her violin longingly, Isa took a deep breath and stared out the window. There wasn't much talking in the van, given that everyone who had been in the tent was now fast asleep. Mama was listening to a news podcast, while Laney was busy cutting out letters that spelled out "Happy Birthday Papa" to paste on the back windows of the van. Though Isa couldn't see it, she imagined that there were hundreds of tiny pieces of paper at Laney's feet. She didn't know what Mr. Ritchie was thinking by lending them his van.

In front of her, Hyacinth was knitting, which Isa found amusing because it was ninety degrees outside. Now Isa's leg was falling asleep. The weight of Jessie's

head was cutting off her circulation.

Ludwig Van pulled off the highway and entered a complex of superstores. There, right in the middle of the massive shopping center, was a Target.

"Target!" Laney shouted.

Oliver and Jessie instantly woke up.

"Did someone say Target?" Oliver said, his hair sticking up after his nap.

"I love Target," Hyacinth said reverently, already packing up her knitting supplies and getting ready to unbuckle her seat belt.

"It's just a Target," Orlando said. "What's the big deal?"

"Target is the best," breathed Hyacinth as Mama parked.

The Vanderbeekers, having lived in New York City all their life, found Target a magical place. They loved how it sold so many things and how the aisles were so wide and clean. It was the opposite of New York City stores, which were often tiny, cramped, and crowded. Isa liked that there was a whole aisle for dental hygiene, while Oliver loved the vast candy selection. Jessie appreciated the assortment of shampoos, as she was always experimenting to find something that would smooth her frizzy hair. Mama was fond of their dish-cloths, which were the most absorbent she had ever tried, and Papa always headed straight toward the men's department to peruse their impressive selection of coveralls. Hyacinth and Laney enjoyed the pet section for its large assortment of fun chew toys.

"Ground rules," Mama said, turning around so she faced her kids. "We only have thirty minutes here. Oliver, you're not allowed to go barefoot inside the store, so you're going to have to wear my extra pair of sneakers."

"Seriously?" Oliver said, horrified at the thought

of wearing his *mom's* shoes.

"Mr. B and Orlando, I can run in and buy you each a pair of cheap flip-flops. Then you can come in and buy your own shoes," Mama continued, ignoring Oliver. "In addition to the shoes, I think we'll need snacks and some camping equipment. Is there anything else we need? Oliver, did you pack underwear?"

"Mama!" Oliver exclaimed, flushing.

"Well, did you?"

"No," he admitted.

It turned out that Laney hadn't packed underwear either. Isa, deciding that this was a good time to get some violin practice in, stayed by the van even though Target and its lovely dental aisle and air-conditioning called to her. Mr. B and Orlando, who had to wait until Mama came back with the flip-flops, stayed with her, pulling the doors to the van open and swinging their bare feet off the side while Isa carefully took out her violin and stood on a grassy patch under a tree. Franz gratefully followed her and plopped down in the shade, panting in the heat. She poured some water into his bowl and set it next to him.

The violin felt good in her hands as she carefully

tuned and adjusted the pegs, then warmed up with scales. And there, in the middle of a superstore parking lot in Ohio, she played, to the wonderment of many passersby. By the time Mama returned with the flip-flops, a few people had paused, listening to her play. One person even threw a dollar bill into her case. Orlando and Mr. B put the flip-flops on and headed into Target, leaving Isa alone to focus on her music. Time passed, and she didn't stop until she heard her family returning.

Her family was a loud bunch, and Isa reluctantly put her violin down and packed it back into the case. She wished she had more practice time. A few scattered strangers clapped for her, and Isa gave them quick smiles.

Then she caught sight of her family.

❂ ❂ ❂

Target was the best place in the world, Laney thought as they walked through the huge store. Not only did it have everything, but there were so many choices for every product! As Mama and Mr. Beiderman compared tent brands, Laney kept her eyes on Jessie and Orlando. She knew they were up to something, and she was going to find out what.

Laney peeked into the next aisle, and there they were in front of some inflatable pillows. But Jessie and Orlando weren't looking at the shelves; they were on their phones, staring at the tiny screens.

"These questions are going to take time," Jessie said.

"Let's write them all down while we have reception. Then we can work on them in the van," Orlando suggested. "I still can't believe this program leads to a full scholarship to Berkeley. I looked it up and they have one of the best programs in the world for biological and biomedical studies."

"Did I tell you Mr. Van Hooten suggested that Isa look at a music conservatory in California too? It's supposed to be a really good school."

"That would be awesome if we all ended up at colleges in the same area," Orlando said.

Laney's breath hitched. *College? California?* An uncomfortable feeling lodged in the pit of her stomach. She knew college was coming in a few years, but she had thought that Jessie and Orlando would go to a school in New York City, like the one Mr. Beiderman or Papa worked at. There were plenty of great schools near their brownstone. Why were they thinking of applying to a school in *California?*

Laney felt sick. She had assumed her older sisters would always be around. She couldn't live without Isa and Jessie! It would be like living without Mama! To top it all off, Orlando was practically their family member. She saw him every day. How could he even think of leaving her?

Laney was still huddled at the end of the aisle when Jessie and Orlando rounded the corner and bumped into her.

"Hey, Laney," Orlando said. "You look tired. Want a piggyback ride to the cash register?"

Laney nodded, and Orlando swung her onto his back. As they made their way to the front of the store, Laney knew that she had to do everything possible to make sure her sisters and Orlando did *not* go to California.

❋ ❋ ❋

The Vanderbeekers wheeled two shopping carts brimming with items back to the van. They had bought another tent, a two-person thing for Orlando and Mr. Beiderman, since it appeared that they would be camping their way across the country and would need more space once they picked up Papa. They'd also bought inflatable camping pillows, thin foam pads in a rainbow of colors to sleep on, an extra tarp, and campfire food, including beans, soup, marshmallows, and hot dogs. Hyacinth had bought two notebooks small enough to fit in her pocket, Oliver had gotten a pair of shoes (and underwear), Laney had gotten a pack of origami paper and an art kit so she had something to do in the car (and underwear), Jessie had purchased a new bottle of anti-frizz shampoo, Mama had gotten a pack of her favorite dish towels, and they had bought Isa a new toothbrush *and* a pack of floss.

Isa, surprised by their many purchases, raised her eyebrows at the sight of her family. But then she saw Mr. Beiderman's shoes and her jaw dropped.

"Wow, Mr. B, I did *not* expect you to choose shoes that color," Isa said, staring at him. His new sneakers were fluorescent yellow.

"It was the only pair in my size," he grumbled.

"It wasn't the *only* pair," Oliver corrected him.

"I personally think you should have gotten the pink ones."

Orlando, who wore a shoe size larger than Mr. B's, had selected black running shoes that looked similar to the ones Rocco had stolen the night before.

Hyacinth looked at Ludwig, then back at the shopping carts. "How are we going to get all that stuff into the van?"

"The tent needs to go on top of the van," Mama said, "and the rest of the stuff needs to somehow fit inside. Please hurry. We still have six more hours of driving before we reach Elberfeld."

They managed to squeeze the new purchases into the van by stashing them under the passenger seats and cramming them into corners. The van took on a decidedly more crowded feel.

"Where is Papa going to sit?" Jessie wondered out loud. There wasn't much space left.

"Speaking of Papa," Isa said, "we should wish him a happy birthday." She got her phone, selected his number, and put it on speaker.

Papa's voice filled the van. "Hi, family!"

"Happy birthday!" they all chorused, and Oliver

began the "fun" birthday song, which involved them singing a jazzed-up version instead of the traditional melody that had been deemed "too depressing" many years ago.

"Thank you!" Papa said when they had finished. "I miss you!"

"We miss you too," everyone chorused.

Papa gave them a quick overview of what he planned to do on his birthday, which included helping Uncle Sylvester mend a fence and clean the chicken house. Then the reception got fuzzy and they had to disconnect.

"He has no idea what we're doing," Hyacinth said happily.

Mama checked her watch. "We've got to go if we want to get to the farm before dinner."

Mr. Beiderman, who was now in the driver's seat and ready to take the next shift, started the engine. It had been so hectic with loading the purchases onto the van and the call with Papa that no one noticed that Laney, usually so chatty and full of energy, had not said a word since leaving Target.

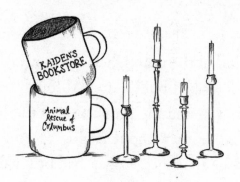

# Five

Hyacinth was very satisfied with her new notebooks, which she stashed in her backpack. Having spent the last few months of third grade studying poetry and song lyrics with her teacher, Ms. Santiago, Hyacinth had tried writing some poetry of her own over the summer. She had filled four notebooks already, and she was almost at the end of the notebook she was currently writing in.

It was good that she had brought her entire savings with her on the trip, and she had a *lot* of money since she had been getting paid all summer to water and weed Jimmy L's mom's garden. Jimmy L, one of Oliver's best friends, lived in the building right behind their brownstone, and their backyards adjoined each other. Earlier in the year, Uncle Arthur, Orlando, Jessie, and Oliver had built a door through the wooden fence that separated the properties so the boys could go back and forth without having to go around the block or scale the fence. Oliver had originally wanted a rope swing that catapulted him from the treehouse to Jimmy L's yard, but Jessie said the physics didn't work out.

Because Ms. Linh worked two jobs, she only had time to work on her garden on the weekends. She paid Hyacinth ten dollars a week to water and weed her vegetable garden from Monday to Friday, which seemed like a lot of money to Hyacinth, who would have done it for free. But Ms. Linh insisted, and Hyacinth had loved tending the garden. Ms. Linh was originally from Vietnam, and she grew some plants that Hyacinth was unfamiliar with: vegetables with hard shells and spikes, leafy greens that grew from sweet potatoes, an herb with red veins called amaranth, and bok choy.

Hyacinth had taken care of the garden since May, only stopping a week ago when Ms. Linh's niece arrived to stay at the Linhs' apartment while Jimmy L was visiting his grandparents in Texas. Ms. Linh's niece took over garden duties, which was good because it meant the garden would be cared for during the Vanderbeekers' road trip. Hyacinth had made a whole $110 for her work.

The van continued along an assortment of highways, traffic easing up the farther they traveled west. They stopped in Cincinnati to pick up lunch at a local deli and ate it outside on the grass of Eden Park. Then they crossed over the Ohio River into Kentucky.

"I didn't know we were going to drive through Kentucky," Hyacinth said.

Mr. Beiderman unfolded a big paper map. "We're only passing through briefly. Let me figure out how

WELCOME TO

# Kentucky
UNBRIDLED SPIRIT

Birthplace of Abraham Lincoln

long. If an inch is equal to fifty miles, then—"

"We'll be here for an hour and a half," Jessie said, consulting the GPS on her phone.

Hyacinth wrote the time, 2:48 p.m., at the top of her journal, along with "A Brief Trip Through Kentucky." She paused, chewed on the eraser of her pencil, then wrote:

*Ninety minutes in Kentucky*
*just passing through.*
*The green is greener here*
*than what I knew, I knew.*

*Ninety minutes in Kentucky*
*how I wish I could*
*spend this time with you.*
*You would love it too.*

*Ninety minutes in Kentucky*
*is coming to an end.*
*Minutes pass by, and*
*I'm closer to you, again.*

Hyacinth hummed as she wrote, the rumble of the car providing enough background noise that no one could hear her. She didn't like singing because then people looked at her and she didn't like people looking at her! No one knew she liked to write down words, as if from a soundtrack in her head, and what she really wanted was a way to make music. None of the Vanderbeekers except Isa had an instrument, although Oliver did occasionally mention that drums would be nice. Their parents always laughed when he said it.

"I think Franz needs to go to the bathroom," Laney announced.

Hyacinth looked at Franz. He was fast asleep, his mouth open and his tongue hanging out of his mouth.

"We just stopped an hour ago," Mama said.

Laney wiggled in her seat. "I think he really needs to go."

Mama sighed. "I'll stop at the next gas station."

A few minutes later, the van turned into a gas station and Laney jumped out and raced for the bathroom, Mama following her. Jessie, Isa, and Oliver wandered into the convenience store to get something to drink. Hyacinth stuffed her notebook into her back pocket, snapped Franz's leash on, and got out of Ludwig, the hot sun beating down on her skin. Mr. B stayed in the van with the air-conditioning running so the cats didn't get too hot. Hyacinth walked Franz to a grassy spot, and Orlando joined her.

The gas station was situated on a street with a small grocery store and a parking lot covered by a tent. Under the tent were lots of tables filled with trinkets and surrounded by larger items, like rocking chairs and high chairs and large planters. A big sign stood outside the tent.

Hyacinth and Orlando wandered over, intrigued.

"What *is* this?" Hyacinth asked as they got closer to the tent.

"Basically it's a yard sale, only instead of having it in your yard, you rent a table and bring the items you want to sell here," Orlando explained. "It's good because shoppers only have to go to one place to look for things, rather than going from home to home. There are lots of these where I lived in Georgia."

"There's something like this in Harlem," Hyacinth said, "in front of the community center. People bring stuff they've made to sell, or they sell things they don't want anymore."

They wandered through the maze of tables looking at all the unusual things. There were creepy dolls, not unlike the ones in the window of the campground they had stayed at, and lots and lots of mugs with different logos and sayings on them. Hyacinth wondered how many mugs there were in the world. Certainly enough for everyone to have at least one hundred! There were beautiful glass candlesticks and old plastic toys and silverware and used books. Then something caught her eye.

As if it had been placed there just for her, a guitar was perched upright on a stand next to a table. Hyacinth walked over, dragging Franz, who had detected that someone in the vicinity was eating something delicious. The guitar wasn't in the best condition; there was rust on the silver pegs and there were dings here and there, but the wood was a gorgeous, warm brown.

"Do you know how to play?" Orlando asked, coming up behind her.

"I know nothing about it," Hyacinth admitted, "but I like guitar music, and sometimes I get music in my head and write words to it."

Orlando raised his eyebrows. "Really? Is that what you're doing in that little notebook you're always scribbling in?"

When Hyacinth nodded, he asked, "Can I see something you've written?"

Hyacinth hesitated. After a moment, remembering that Orlando was one of the nicest human beings on the planet and would never make fun of her, she pulled out her notebook and flipped it to the page with the Kentucky lyrics on it.

Orlando was silent as he read it. Then he looked at her and said, "Do you have a melody you've been thinking about with this?"

Hyacinth nodded. She started humming it quietly.

A man wearing a white T-shirt and blue jeans rambled over to the table, and Hyacinth instantly went quiet. He was bald but had a face full of silver whiskers. "Can I help you?" he asked.

"No," Hyacinth said at the same time Orlando said "Yes."

"Would it be possible for us to look at the guitar?" Orlando asked.

"Sure thing," the man said, taking the guitar off the stand and passing it over the table. "It's a travel guitar, so it's smaller than a traditional acoustic guitar."

Orlando held it and strummed some chords.

"You play the guitar?" Hyacinth asked. How did she not know that?

"I had one back in Georgia," Orlando said. "My cousin taught me to play a little, but I couldn't bring it with me when I left the apartment."

Hyacinth thought back to the day when she had realized that Orlando was no longer living where she thought he lived. They had gone to his building only to find two guys emptying everything from the apartment and tossing it all into a dumpster.

"Maybe you should get a guitar," Hyacinth said.

Orlando continued to play, the sound drifting through the tent and causing shoppers and vendors to look over in appreciation.

"It's got some wear and tear, but that's all cosmetic," the vendor said when Orlando stopped playing. "You can't beat that sound."

"I think you should get it," Hyacinth said.

"I think *you* should get it," Orlando said, handing it to her.

"Me!" squeaked Hyacinth. She backed away. "I don't even know how to play!"

"Just hold it," Orlando said. "You don't have to play anything." He took Franz's leash from her.

She held the guitar the way Orlando had. It felt clunky in her hands, but it also felt solid and reassuring against her body. Experimentally, she strummed it. The notes rang out, and even though she hadn't even played a tune, the sound made her breathless.

"How much?" Orlando asked the vendor.

"Twenty," the man said around his toothpick. "You can have the stand and a gig bag. I think I have a chord book around here if you want it."

"Twenty dollars?" Hyacinth asked, her mouth falling open. She couldn't believe she could afford a *guitar!*

The man shrugged. "If that's too much, I'll take

fifteen. I've been lugging that guitar around with me for four months and no one's been interested. I bought it for my son years ago, but he never got into it. I would be glad if you took it off my hands."

"I'll take it," Hyacinth breathed, then looked at Orlando. "Unless you want it?"

"No way," Orlando said. "It's yours. In any case, when I get another guitar, it will be a full-sized one. I'm too big to play that little travel guitar."

Hyacinth handed the guitar back to the vendor so he could put it in the bag and sift through the stack of books on the table for the chord book.

"This is fun," said Orlando, looking happy.

"Now we need to find a guitar for you," Hyacinth said as she gave the vendor twenty dollars and he handed over the guitar in its bag, the stand, the chord book, and a jar full of picks. "You're the one who knows how to play."

"Molly over there is selling a guitar," the man said, pointing to a woman sitting behind a table filled with mugs.

"Thanks," Orlando said. "We'll take a look."

And that is why, when Jessie tracked them down

ten minutes later, annoyed because they'd needed to be back on the road fifteen minutes ago, both Hyacinth and Orlando had guitars in their hands and big smiles on their faces.

# Six

Oliver stood by the van, sweating. Kentucky sure was hot! He could see Hyacinth and Orlando over at the flea market, but he was too lazy to walk over and see what they were doing. Laney was rolling a cold bottle of water over her forehead, and Mama was on the phone with Auntie Harrigan, reminding her to pay the bakery's electricity bill.

Mr. B was checking his watch. "We need to get going."

Jessie ran over to collect Hyacinth and Orlando, and a minute later the three of them were walking back to the van, Hyacinth and Orlando both carrying something on their shoulders.

"You bought *guitars?*" Oliver said, incredulous.

"Orlando said he would teach me," Hyacinth said.

"You had enough money for that?" Oliver asked.

"Mine was only twenty dollars!" Hyacinth said.

Oliver was jealous. He sort of wanted to go over to the flea market too and see what he could get for twenty dollars, but Mr. B was ushering them into the van. Oliver looked at his mom, who was still on the phone, wondering what she would say to these new purchases, but she only smiled distractedly at Hyacinth while continuing to give Auntie Harrigan a list of things to do at the bakery.

Orlando climbed into the last row and Hyacinth settled down in the second row with her guitar, the chord book open in front of her. Oliver squished himself into his seat, his feet resting on the cat carrier, and leaned his head back. Behind him, he could hear Hyacinth flipping through the guitar book and plucking the different strings. Way in the back of the van, Orlando and Jessie were working on something, but he couldn't tell what. Between the soft strumming and the rumble of low voices and the heat, Oliver soon drifted off to sleep. When he woke up, the van was pulled over on the side of the highway. He was sticky with sweat and his mouth was dry.

"What's going on?" he asked, disoriented.

"Ludwig is overheating," Jessie said, looking at her phone. "The air conditioner started getting weaker and there was this clicking sound, and now look." She pointed out the front window. Steam was billowing from the front of the van.

"Is the van going to blow up?" Laney asked, unbuckling and grabbing Tuxedo's carrying case. She climbed over Oliver, pulled open the van door, jumped out, and ran into the field.

"Everything is fine," Mama said. "I think the engine just needs to cool down. We've been driving all day in one-hundred-degree heat. Jessie, can you call Triple A?"

Oliver hopped out of the van, hoping there was a breeze outside. There wasn't. Mr. B was already out, looking at the hood.

"Should I open it?" he asked Oliver.

"I don't know," Oliver said. "It looks really hot. You should probably leave it alone."

"Good idea," Mr. B said, relieved. "I haven't owned a car in decades. I have no idea what I'm doing."

Jessie got out and pressed her phone to her ear. "We are half an hour southeast of Cincinnati, on Interstate 71," Jessie said. "I think we have an overheated engine."

There was a pause; then Jessie said, "Really? That long?" A moment later, she said, "Yeah, that makes sense." Then she recited the license plate number and hung up.

"Two hours at least," Jessie said, looking around. There wasn't much to see except a barn and a farmhouse in the distance.

"It's so hot," Oliver said, pulling his shirt away from his skin. He checked his watch. It was almost four-thirty. "How far away is Elberfeld?"

Jessie checked her phone. "Over two hours."

Oliver did a quick calculation. "So that means if our car gets fixed in two hours, then we'll be there around eight-thirty or nine. That's still okay, right?"

"It will take two hours just for Triple A to get here," Jessie said. "Then they'll probably need to tow the van to a mechanic's shop."

"So that means we won't see Papa today," Oliver said flatly. "That was the whole point of driving all this way!" He looked around. The highway was long and lonely, and the few cars that passed were speeding toward their destination, not interested in assisting a broken-down van.

Laney had run about fifty yards away from the van and taken a seat on the dry grass, the cat carrier in her lap. When she saw Oliver looking at her, she yelled, "Is it going to blow up?"

"No!" Oliver yelled. "Come back!"

But Laney just shook her head, looking warily at the steam coming from the van.

Jessie wandered over to talk to Mama and Mr. Beiderman about what they should do. Oliver wiped his brow, then took a slug from his canteen only to remember that he should probably save his water. Worried about Peaches and Cream, he pulled the crate out of the van, trying to stay within the shade made by the vehicle.

Oliver couldn't believe there was so much land and no one around. In New York City, there were people everywhere you looked. Isa, Orlando, and Hyacinth had taken their instruments out of the van, worried about the heat damaging the wood, and they all stood there, sweating and waiting for the AAA truck.

When would it come?

❖ ❖ ❖

Laney didn't know why people weren't joining her at a safe distance from the van. She didn't want to get blown up, no sir. By the van, Franz panted, while Hyacinth occasionally rubbed him down with water from her bottle.

She was worried about the pets. They had so much fur, and being inside the crates was probably super uncomfortable. It was so hot that the air seemed to shimmer. She looked into the distance, where she could see a farmhouse. It looked far away, like it would take her five whole days to walk there. The grass was really tall and made her legs itch.

A dark dot in the distance seemed to move, and Laney rubbed her eyes, wondering if she was hallucinating. She knew this was something that happened to people who were stuck in the desert for days—she had read about it in a book. She kept looking at the black dot, which appeared to be getting bigger and bigger. Isa and

Oliver joined her, curious about what was approaching.

Pretty soon, the black dot turned into what looked like a horse galloping in their direction. A minute later, Laney saw that it *was* a horse, and someone was riding it. A minute later, she could see that not only was a person riding it, but the person was a *girl* who didn't look much older than she was.

"Hi," the girl said when she got close, the horse slowing down to a walk. "Your car break down?"

"Yes," Laney said. "We're stuck for another couple of hours until Triple A comes."

"That's happened to us before," the girl said. "I saw the smoke in the distance, so I decided to investigate. I'm Lucie."

"I'm Laney," Laney said. "And this is Isa and Oliver."

"Hey," Isa and Oliver said.

"Is that your horse?" Laney asked.

"Yep," Lucie said. "His name is Pineapple."

"Wow," Laney said, impressed. "I wish I had a horse, but we don't have enough space for one. I have a cat and a bunny, though." She held up the carrier so

Lucie could get a peek at Tuxedo.

"So cute!" Lucie said. "I want a rabbit, but my parents say no." Lucie looked past Laney. The rest of the Vanderbeekers, Orlando, and Mr. B were all standing by the van staring at Pineapple with interest. "That your family?" she asked.

"Yes," Laney said. "Plus two of our best friends. We're trying to get to our dad in Elberfeld because it's his birthday today. His flight got canceled, so he couldn't get back home. We live in New York City."

Now it was Lucie's turn to be impressed. "New York City?" she asked. "I've always wanted to go there! Do you see Broadway musicals all the time?"

Laney giggled. "No. I've only seen two."

Lucie sighed. "I want to ride on the subway and see a Broadway show. Are you all going to wait out here until a tow truck comes?"

"Yeah," Laney said, then glanced at the carrier. "Although I'm worried Tuxedo will get really hot."

Lucie reached a hand to her waist and grabbed what looked like a walkie-talkie. "Chris? Can you come here with the truck? I just met some people with an overheated van." The device crackled and Laney thought she could hear someone respond, but it was so garbled she couldn't tell what the person said. Lucie hooked the walkie-talkie back on her waistband. "Chris is going to help."

A minute later, a vehicle was heading their way, puffs of dust all around it.

Mama, Mr. Beiderman, Orlando, and the rest of Laney's siblings came over to say hi to Pineapple. By the time Laney introduced everyone to Lucie, the truck had arrived. Inside was the youngest driver Laney had ever seen.

"Is that your *dad?*" Laney said, amazed.

"My dad?" Lucie hooted with laughter. "That's my brother! He's twelve!"

"He can *drive?*" Oliver asked, eyes wide.

"Just around the farm," Lucie said. "He's not old enough to get a license, but he can drive on the property. He has to sit on an old phone book to see out the windshield, and we attached wood blocks to the pedals so he can reach them."

The Vanderbeekers couldn't believe it. A twelve-year-old driving a pickup truck! He stopped the vehicle next to Pineapple and Lucie, then stuck his head out the window.

"Want a ride to the house while you're waiting for your tow?" he hollered. "It's too hot to be outside!"

The Vanderbeekers looked at Mama, who looked at Mr. B, who looked at the twelve-year-old driver.

"I think I should stay with the van," Mr. B said. "In case Triple A gets here early. We really need to get to Elberfeld today."

"Just call Triple A and tell them you're staying in a house five minutes away," Lucie advised. "Ask them to call when they're on their way. Chris can drive you back."

Mr. Beiderman nodded, not seeing fault with the plan. So Jessie called AAA and was assured that the mechanic would contact them when he was on his way, while Isa, Hyacinth, and Orlando grabbed their instruments and locked up the van. Everyone except Mr. Beiderman piled into the bed of the truck. Mr. B climbed into the passenger seat next to Chris. Oliver kept his hand on the crate holding Peaches and Cream, and Laney balanced Tuxedo's carrier on her lap. Franz, thrilled by the experience, hung his front paws over the edge of the truck bed, the wind blowing his ears back as he howled with happiness. Pineapple and Lucie trotted ahead of the pickup toward the house and all the while Laney wondered at this magical farm where kids could ride horses and drive trucks.

# Seven

The past twenty-four hours had been a lesson in trust, Jessie thought as she bumped along in the back of a pickup truck driven by a twelve-year-old she had just met ten minutes earlier. In front of them was Lucie riding Pineapple, looking as if she had been riding horses since she was two years old. It made Jessie wonder what she and her siblings would be like if they had grown up in the middle of the country instead of in a huge city. Would Laney have a horse? Would Oliver be driving a pickup truck?

A few minutes later, they passed under a sign that said ROCKING HORSE RANCH and arrived at the house, a rambling home painted light blue with white trim. Next to the farmhouse was a red barn with a gleaming silver silo. It was as if they had stepped right into the picture that came up on the internet when you searched for "American farm."

A woman emerged from the house, a large black dog wagging his tail at her feet. "Hello, friends!" she called.

"Hello!" everyone said back to her as they scrambled out of the truck.

"I heard you had some bad luck on the road. I'm Sue, Lucie and Chris's mom," the woman said as the Vanderbeekers, Mr. B, and Orlando gathered around her and introduced themselves.

"I hope we're not being a burden," Mama said.

"Not at all!" Sue said. "Do you want me to reach out to some mechanics?"

"Thank you, but Triple A should be here soon," Mama replied. "We're all set."

"Want to help me put Pineapple back in her stall?" Lucie asked Laney as she dismounted.

After Mama confirmed that this was okay, Laney yelped with happiness, and the two girls headed for the barn while everyone else followed Sue into the house. Franz beelined for Sue's dog, and pretty soon they were racing around the house as if they had been best friends since the beginning of time.

Jessie loved the farmhouse. Giant windows lined every wall, filling the house with light. They entered through the kitchen, which was spacious and cheerful. A big farm sink, currently filled with ripe tomatoes, was in front of a window overlooking the farm. On the stove were big pots filled with water, steam rising from them. Copper and steel pots and pans hung from a rack suspended above a large island in the middle of the room. Nestled into a corner window was a small table covered with a yellow tablecloth printed with daisies.

"What a beautiful kitchen!" Mama exclaimed as she walked around.

"Mom's in here all the time. Her peach jam has won first prize at the County Fair for the last five years running," Chris said as he grabbed a doughnut off the counter and shoved it into his mouth. Oliver observed this, then followed suit.

"Here, take a couple of jars with you," Sue said, pulling open a pantry that was filled with hundreds of Bell jars containing a rainbow of items.

"Wow, what *is* all that?" Jessie asked.

"Tomatoes, apple pie filling, jalapeño jelly, candied jalapeños, peach jam, strawberry jam, apple butter, green beans, corn cob honey, spaghetti sauce, sweet corn, dill pickles, bread and butter pickles, corn relish, and peaches," Sue said proudly, pointing as she named them. "I'm canning some tomatoes right now."

"I can help," Mama said.

"Me too," Hyacinth said.

Sue laughed. "My kids sure did pick up the right people from the side of the road! I won't say no to help, but only if you help yourself to some lemonade first. I'm assuming you've been on the road all day?"

While Mama explained where they were from, where they were headed, and why, Sue poured tall glasses of cold lemonade. After Isa inquired about possible places to practice her violin, Chris showed her the living room before running off with Oliver.

"Do you mind if we work on our science project paper?" Jessie asked Sue.

"Sure," she said, pointing to the kitchen table. "Make yourself at home."

Jessie and Orlando settled down at the big wooden

table and took out their notebooks. Sue, figuring Mr. Beiderman might want a job after watching him fidget uncomfortably in the corner, suggested he go to the barn, where her husband was doing chores. Mr. B left, eager to be useful.

Meanwhile, Mama and Hyacinth got a lesson on canning.

"I'm just sterilizing some quart jars"—Sue pointed to the oven—"and the lids," she said, pointing to a pot of simmering water. "The tomatoes are washed but need to be cut like this." She demonstrated by cutting an X at the top of a tomato.

Hyacinth stood by the sink and started cutting the tomatoes and putting them in a steel bowl. Mama and Sue would occasionally dump them into pots of boiling water, then remove them after sixty seconds to cool down so they could take the skins off. After that, they filled each hot, sterilized jar with peeled tomatoes and a little bit of concentrated lemon juice for acidity, then wiped the rims clean and put the sterilized lids and rings on.

The jars were then put into a hot-water bath and brought to a boil, and Sue set a timer for eighty-five minutes. Hyacinth listened to Mama and Sue chat about their unexpected road trip. Sue shared about growing up in Kentucky and what life was like on a farm.

Meanwhile, Isa practiced her violin, the beautiful music drifting through the farmhouse.

"She is *so* talented!" Sue gushed. "I tried to get my kids to play the piano, but they had no interest. They just wanted to be outside, messing around in the dirt or playing with the animals."

Done cutting the tomatoes, Hyacinth went to sit with Jessie and Orlando, who were huddled over their notebooks.

"What are you doing?" she asked.

Jessie looked up. "Oh, just some work for Ms. Brown for the Science and Engineering Fair."

Hyacinth nodded and left them to their work—it looked very intense—but something felt weird about Jessie's response. She thought about it when she poured herself another glass of lemonade, trying to replay the moment in her mind again. After some thought, she realized what was wrong. When Jessie responded to her question, she hadn't quite looked at Hyacinth's face. Jessie *always* looked directly at someone when she talked to them. Isa tended to look off to the side at different points during a conversation, but Jessie never did . . . until just now.

The sound of a grandfather clock chiming six times interrupted Hyacinth's musings. It was six o'clock and there was still no word from AAA.

Papa's birthday was six hours from being over, and they had no way to get to him.

✵ ✵ ✵

Laney loved the farm, she loved Lucie, and she loved Pineapple. In the barn, there was another horse, named Moonlight, as well as a cow named Calvin, three pigs, and a goat. In the paddock adjoining the barn was a llama named Michelle O'Llama, who was keeping watch over a herd of ducks. There was also a chicken coop and at least thirty chickens of various breeds pecking the grass.

The barn was cool and smelled good, like earth and hay and animals. Inside, Lucie's dad was fixing the barn wall, which had been damaged in a recent storm. Lucie introduced Laney, and then they took care of Pineapple. Lucie removed Pineapple's saddle and bridle and showed Laney how to brush the horse. Then they led Pineapple to her water trough. While Pineapple was drinking, Lucie pulled out a hose and swiveled the nozzle so water came pouring out. "This is to cool her off, since it's so hot today. Want to try?" She passed the hose to Laney.

"She likes getting hosed down?" Laney asked.

"Yep," Lucie said as they sprayed water on her. Pineapple tossed her head back with glee. When they were done, Lucie led Pineapple into her stall and dumped a big clump of hay into a basket hanging on the door.

"Want to see the hayloft?" Lucie asked.

"Sure," Laney said. "Do you have a rope swing?" She knew all about haylofts and rope swings from reading *Charlotte's Web.*

"We do!"

The girls raced to the other side of the barn, where a single, heavy rope hung from the ceiling. Lucie grabbed it and scrambled up the piles of hay.

"Watch me!" Lucie called, then flung herself into the air. After she landed, she handed the rope to

Laney, who followed Lucie's path up the hay bales, grabbed the rope with both hands, and jumped. After a few turns each, they sank into the hay, catching their breath.

"You're so lucky you get to go to California," Lucie said. "I've never been there. I would love to see the Pacific Ocean."

"Yeah," Laney replied, suddenly remembering the whole college situation.

"You don't seem excited," Lucie observed.

Laney told Lucie about what she had learned from spying on Jessie and Orlando in Target. "I never thought they were thinking about going to college so far away."

Lucie nodded. "I don't know why anyone would want to leave home for college. I'm going to stay living on the farm forever. Did you know that most people settle down in the place they went to college?"

"Really?" Laney asked.

"Yep," Lucie said. "I've seen it a hundred times. All my cousins ended up living in the same town where they went to college: Boston, Miami, Denver, Los Angeles. Once they went to college, they didn't even come home for summers. When I was little, our family gatherings were huge. But now no one shows up. They all moved away."

Laney's stomach dropped at the thought of her sisters and Orlando going to college and never coming back home. The brownstone would never be the same.

Laney swallowed. "What do you think I should do?"

"You could talk to them," Lucie suggested. "Tell them you don't want them to leave."

Laney shook her head. "I'm not even supposed to know they're applying for this scholarship. They're keeping everything a secret."

"They can only go if they get the scholarship, right?" Lucie said.

Laney nodded.

"Then you have to make sure they don't get their applications in."

Laney's eyes widened. "That's a good idea!"

Lucie checked her watch. "It's after six o'clock. Maybe you can stay for dinner!"

"Maybe," Laney said, thinking about Papa. If they stayed for dinner, would that mean they were giving up on trying to get to Elberfeld today?

Then Mr. B came into the barn.

"I just got the call!" he said. "Triple A is on their way!"

"Drat," Lucie said. "I wanted you to stay longer."

They met everyone else at the pickup truck, only this time, Sue drove, while Chris and Oliver, now fast friends, sat in the back of the truck and talked about their favorite basketball players. Mama got in the front passenger seat, so Mr. B had to sit in the back. The truck bumped along the field and arrived back at the van just as the tow truck appeared.

"Thank you for hosting us!" Mama said, a big box of canned tomatoes, peach jam, and apple pie filling in her arms. "And thank you for the food. You are too generous."

"I want to visit them in New York City," Lucie told her mom.

"You're welcome to visit us anytime," Mama told Sue. "Really."

Sue, Chris, and Lucie watched as the two AAA employees analyzed Ludwig and hooked the van up to their tow truck. Three people could fit in the tow truck, and a second AAA vehicle came down the road to pick the rest of them up. The Vanderbeekers, along with their three cats, one dog, one violin, and two guitars, were finally off to the mechanic's shop.

Laney waved out the window at her new friends, and when she could no longer see them, she looked at the car dashboard. It was seven o'clock.

Elberfeld was two hours away. Was it still possible to get the car fixed and be in Elberfeld in time for Papa's birthday?

# Eight

The AAA vehicle following the tow truck to the mechanic's shop was not comfortable, Isa thought as they bumped along the highway back toward Cincinnati. The seats were so worn down that the leather was ripped; yellow foam bled out and exposed coils jabbed into her thigh. She was never going to complain about Ludwig again.

An hour later, they arrived at a shop called Al's Automotive. It was late by then—almost eight o'clock—and it looked as if the shop was closed. The gates were pulled down and the neon sign was turned off. The van driver knocked on the door, and a moment later, the Vanderbeekers heard it unlock and then open.

"What?" said the man, who was wearing a mechanic's shirt with the name "Al" stitched on it.

"This is the tow that was called in late this afternoon," the van driver said. "We were told to bring it here."

Al shook his head. "I'm closed for the night. Just about to head home and eat dinner with my wife."

The Vanderbeekers looked at each other. Surely this didn't mean they would have to stay overnight in Cincinnati, when Papa was a mere three hours away?

Fred the tow truck driver looked conflicted. He didn't seem to want to abandon them at the mechanic's shop with a van that needed servicing, but he also needed to get to his next job.

"You said you would take the job," Fred said. "What am I supposed to do with these people?"

"You were two hours late," Al said. "I can get to it on Monday."

"Monday!" the Vanderbeekers, Mr. B, and Orlando yelped. That was two whole days away!

"Just because you have an emergency doesn't mean I need to move around my whole schedule," Al said with a shrug. "I'm sorry, but if I responded to every emergency, I would never have a day off."

Isa sort of understood what he was saying, but she also wished he had someone working for him who *could* respond to these types of emergencies. Like when a vanload of people drove over ten hours and nearly six hundred and fifty miles in twenty-four hours and slept at a creepy campground just to find out that they weren't going to be able to spend their father's fortieth birthday with him after all.

Al closed the door, locked it, and then must have exited through the back door, because a minute later they saw him in a black Jeep, zipping out of the lot and onto the street.

"So, uh, I guess you'll find a place to stay the night?" Fred said.

Mama sighed as she took her phone out and looked up lodging nearby.

They watched the tow truck lower Ludwig's front wheels to the ground. Fred unhooked all the cables that attached it to the truck and wished them luck before they headed to their next assignment.

"Maybe Uncle Sylvester or Aunt Sabine can come get us? We're only two hours away," Isa suggested.

"They don't have a van big enough for all of us," Mama said.

It was getting dark. The Vanderbeekers, defeated, sat down on the curb in the parking lot under a sputtering streetlamp. Jessie's phone was dead, so only Mama could search for lodging. The only option within walking distance was a motel down the street that had gotten 232 one-star reviews. Isa peeked at the photos. The motel looked seriously creepy, as if it could be a place from a Halloween movie set.

Next to her, Laney and Hyacinth were sniffling, and Oliver was jamming his sneaker down on a pebble, trying to crush it into powder. Mr. B was also on his phone, attempting to find another mechanic in the area who could help at such a late hour. Orlando was pacing the parking lot, his arms crossed over his chest.

An hour later, Mama sighed and put her phone down. "I'm going to try to find a cab that can take us to a motel. We're going to have to spend the night in Cincinnati."

Laney and Hyacinth started crying in earnest at her words. Papa's birthday plan was completely ruined.

❖ ❖ ❖

While everyone processed the news that they were going to spend the night in a cramped, crowded van, a truck pulled into the parking lot, headlights flashing into their eyes. Oliver squinted, trying to make out the person inside.

The window rolled down, and a familiar face leaned out. "Need some help?"

Oliver couldn't believe his eyes. The driver was Sue! Chris jumped out from the passenger seat, along with a man who looked to be Mr. Beiderman's age. The man was carrying a big toolbox and a blue gallon jug. After him came Lucie, who immediately ran to Laney and started talking a mile a minute.

"This is Mr. Williams," Chris said. "He used to live next to us and fix all our farm vehicles, but he moved to Cincinnati a year ago."

"We thought you were all set up with a mechanic, or we would have told you about him this afternoon."

Mr. Williams bowed slightly, then pointed to Ludwig Van. "That it?"

Mama nodded, amazed.

"How did you know we needed help?" Oliver asked Chris.

"My mom texted your mom to make sure you made it here safely, and your mom said you were stranded," Chris said. "So we jumped in the truck right away. We were annoyed with ourselves for not telling you to see Mr. Williams in the first place! We called him, and he said he wasn't doing anything but watching the Nature Channel and he would be happy to help. So we picked him up, and here we are!"

"You are a lifesaver," Mama said to Sue. "I don't know how to repay you."

"Oh, please," Sue said, waving a hand in the air. "We couldn't just abandon you in the middle of Cincinnati when you have somewhere to be!"

Oliver and Chris wandered over to Ludwig, where Mr. Williams had already checked on the engine.

"Hold this flashlight for me?" Mr. Williams asked Chris. "Shine it right here."

Chris took the flashlight, and they watched as Mr. Williams inspected the engine. A few minutes later, he stood up and wiped his oily hands on a cloth he took from his toolbox.

"Good news," he reported. "No engine damage. This van is actually in great condition."

"We're borrowing it from a friend who's a mechanic," Oliver told him.

"Your mom was smart to pull over as soon as she knew there was a problem," he told Oliver. "The van is low on coolant, so I'll just fill it up and you can get on your way."

"Really?" Oliver said. "We don't have to spend the night here?"

"Really," Mr. Williams said. He went back to Sue's truck and returned with a blue jug. He popped off the top of a yellow cap in the engine that said "Engine Coolant." He poured the liquid in, then replaced the cap. "All done!"

Mama, who had come over with Sue, said, "That's it? Everything is fine now?"

"This van is ready to roll," Mr. Williams said with a smile. He wiped his hands on a rag he pulled out of his pocket.

Mama fumbled with her bag. "What can we pay you?" she asked, rummaging for her wallet.

Mr. Williams held up a hand. "Happy to help a

friend of Sue's," he said. "She brings enough fresh veggies from her garden and canned goods to keep me well fed. Helping you just means that Sue might bring me one of her famous apple pies the next time she's in town."

"I'm bringing apple pie *and* peach pie next time," Sue promised.

"Sounds good to me," Mr. Williams said. "Now I've got to get back home. The Nature Channel is doing a whole series on animals of Australia, and I don't want to miss the episode on wombats."

"I can't thank you enough," Mama said to Sue and Mr. Williams, enfolding each of them in a hug.

Sue, Chris, Lucie, and Mr. Williams climbed back into the truck while the Vanderbeekers, Mr. B, and Orlando got settled in the van. Mama started the engine, which roared to life as if the steam coming out of the hood had never happened, and they followed Sue's truck out of the parking lot. It turned out that Mr. Williams's house was on the way to the highway, so they waved and yelled "Thank you!" out the window as Sue dropped him off, and then continued following Sue's truck back onto the highway until she took an off-ramp an hour later.

The Vanderbeekers were getting closer to Elberfeld, and the sky was now dark and the air cooler. They opened the windows, the breeze a welcome relief after the heat of the day. It was now nine-thirty, and as long as there weren't any new emergencies, they were only two hours from Elberfeld. Oliver looked at his watch, then looked out the window. Spread across the sky were millions of stars.

"Wow," Oliver said. "Look at the sky!"

The Vanderbeekers, Mr. B, and Orlando craned their necks to look up, amazed at the sight. In New York City, they were lucky to spot a few stars. Here, it

was as if someone had tossed up handfuls of glitter in the air and the sparkles remained suspended in the universe.

The sky was so mesmerizing that Oliver continued to look out the window even as his siblings fell asleep. Next to him, Laney had curled up with Tuxedo in the crook of her neck. In the row behind him, Hyacinth had fallen asleep with her head against the window, Franz snoring next to her. The next thing he knew, the van was slowing down and Mr. Beiderman and Mama were talking.

"I think it's that path," he said. "Yes, I see the sign. Harris Farm."

The van turned onto a graveled lane, then stopped.

"Kids," Mama said softly. "We're here."

Oliver blinked and glanced at his watch. It was eleven-forty-five, fifteen minutes before Papa's birthday was over. He pulled open the van door and watched as a light flickered on in the Harris home. And then the front door opened and Papa's silhouette filled the doorway. A millisecond later, everyone was leaping out of the van and there was hugging and cheering and lots of confetti thrown by Laney.

And when the Vanderbeekers explained what would come next, how they planned a whole road trip based on a promise that Pop-Pop had made twenty years ago, and showed Papa the letter that had started the whole adventure, Papa hugged everyone again, tears streaming down his cheeks as they celebrated in the inky darkness, a glitter-filled sky twinkling above them.

# SUNDAY, AUGUST 10

Miles to Monterey: 2,226

# Nine

When Hyacinth woke up on Sunday morning, she found Sabine, Uncle Sylvester and Aunt Amelia's daughter, sitting in a rocking chair right next to the bed she was sleeping in. She hadn't seen her cousin when they'd arrived the night before because it had been so late. She had taken the bottom bunk in Sabine's room—Sabine slept on the top—and she'd been too tired to feel awkward about sleeping in a bunk with someone she hadn't seen in years.

"I've been waiting and waiting for you to wake up!" Sabine told her, jumping out of the rocking chair and plopping down next to her.

Hyacinth rubbed her eyes. Franz was sprawled across her legs, wagging his tail but making no attempt to move. He was probably tired from all the traveling too. Sabine was wearing jeans with holes in the knees, a green T-shirt that said "Elberfeld 4-H Club," and clunky yellow rubber boots. Her hair was pulled into a sloppy ponytail that trailed all the way down to her waist.

Even though Hyacinth and Sabine had been friends in the past, Hyacinth felt a little shy and uncertain. It had been a long time since they'd hung out. Thankfully, Sabine had no reservations and was now lying on the bed, petting Franz behind his ears as he woofed in happiness.

"I have so much to show you," Sabine told Hyacinth. "We just got some new chickens! Do you want to see? Also, I have a goat named Chocolate Chip. And the ground cherries are in season, and there are so many of them and Mom says we can eat as many as we want!"

Hyacinth was very interested in meeting the new chickens and the goat named Chocolate Chip, so she got out of bed. She wanted to brush her teeth before going anywhere, so Sabine gave her the new toothbrush she had brought home from a recent dentist's visit, which was good because Hyacinth had no idea where her bag was. She was wearing the same clothes she had worn the day before. Sabine offered Hyacinth a pair of her overall shorts and a purple tank top.

"I love these," Hyacinth said when she came out of the bathroom after brushing her teeth and putting on Sabine's clothes. "I've never worn overalls before."

"You've never worn overalls?" Sabine asked, shocked.

"Maybe when I was really little," Hyacinth said. "But I don't remember."

"Are you hungry?" Sabine asked.

Franz woofed.

"Oh, I know *you* are!" Sabine said to Franz, petting his head. "Let's get you some food."

Downstairs in the kitchen, Hyacinth found Papa and Mama sitting on stools at the kitchen island as Uncle Sylvester and Aunt Amelia bustled around the stove making breakfast. It was strange to see Mama relaxing and not taking control of the kitchen.

As if Mama could sense that Hyacinth was there, she swiveled on her stool. "Hi, sweetie! These two won't let me do anything to help. Can you believe it?"

"I'm saving you for something bigger," Aunt Amelia said with a wink. She turned to Hyacinth. "How did you sleep?"

"She was so tired!" Sabine reported. "I've already fed the chickens, watered the garden, and cleaned Chocolate Chip's pen!"

"Well, little miss," Aunt Amelia said to Sabine, cuffing her lightly on the shoulder, "Hyacinth has been on the road for two days and didn't get to bed until after midnight. I think she deserved to sleep in."

Hyacinth took the stool next to Papa. He put an arm around her and pulled her close for a hug. "I've missed you. I still can't believe you came all the way to Elberfeld to pick me up."

"We've got so many plans for you," Hyacinth said.

"I've heard," Papa said. "Thank goodness my boss is okay with me taking so much time off. August is our slowest month." Papa was a computer technician and worked for a big university in the city. "I can't wait to see what you've got planned."

While Hyacinth fed Franz, Laney came downstairs, dragging a disheveled Oliver with her. She beelined straight for Hyacinth.

"Vanderbeeker sibling meeting, *now*," Laney said, grabbing Hyacinth's arm with her free hand.

"Okay, but why—" Hyacinth began, before she was pulled out the door and into the side yard.

"I can come too, right?" Sabine called.

Hyacinth found herself tugged all the way over to the goat enclosure, where Chocolate Chip stared at them with hopeful eyes.

"This is a sibling meeting," Laney informed Sabine as she looked around for anyone who might overhear them.

"What about Jessie and Isa?" Oliver asked.

"Please can I stay?" Sabine said.

Laney crossed her arms over her chest and looked at Sabine. "Fine, but you can't say *anything* to *anyone* about what we talk about."

Sabine spit on her right palm and held it out to Laney.

"Yuck," Oliver said.

"It's a spit swear!" Sabine said. "It means I can't ever break the promise."

Laney held up her pinky. "How about pinky swear instead?"

Sabine shrugged. "Up to you, but a spit swear is more binding."

They hooked pinkies, and Laney seemed satisfied that Sabine was trustworthy.

"Jessie and Orlando are up to something," Laney announced.

"I think so too!" Hyacinth exclaimed. "Jessie lied to me yesterday! She said she was working on something for the science fair, but her eyes were all shifty."

"Can you get to the point?" Oliver asked irritably, glancing back at the house. "Breakfast is almost ready."

"Jessie and Orlando are applying for some big scholarship to go to college," Laney said, then paused dramatically. "In *California!*"

"California!" Hyacinth squeaked.

"Lucky!" Sabine said. "I've always wanted to go to California!"

"So what?" Oliver said with a yawn.

"And I heard them say that Isa was thinking about a school in California too!" Laney reported.

"Not Isa too!" Hyacinth cried.

"You knew they were planning on going to college,

right?" Oliver said.

"I thought they were going to college in *New York City*, not thousands of miles away!" Laney cried. "And once they leave, they'll never come back. They'll end up loving California and staying there permanently."

"Which college is this for?" Oliver asked.

"A place called Bartley. Or is it Barkley?"

"I've never heard of that school," Oliver said, "but I assumed they would go away for college. Then I could have their room."

"*What?*" Laney said. "They're supposed to go to college in New York City! There are so many colleges by us! Why would they want to go all the way to California?"

Oliver looked at the house longingly. "Do you think breakfast is ready?"

"This is more important than food, Oliver," Laney scolded him.

"I can't think when I'm hungry," Oliver said. "Let's talk about this later, okay?"

Hyacinth watched him jog toward the house, then turned to Laney. Her little sister looked crushed, and Hyacinth couldn't blame her. She couldn't imagine living in the brownstone without her older siblings—it just wouldn't be the same.

"You'll help, right?" Laney asked.

"Of course," Hyacinth said automatically. "Wait, what are you thinking about doing?"

"We need to stop Jessie and Orlando from submitting those applications, obviously," Laney said.

"And how are we going to do that?" Sabine asked.

"I don't know," Laney said, "but I am not letting them move. I don't care how great Barkley is."

⚘ ⚘ ⚘

After breakfast, Laney, Hyacinth, and Sabine set out across the farm to Sabine's favorite tree. Completely uninterested in their schemes, Oliver went off with Uncle Sylvester, who was going to teach him how to ride a dirt bike.

Tuxedo, Chocolate Chip, a portly pig named Lady Lollipop, and a chicken that Sabine had named Ramona Quimby, a cute little thing with lots of fluffy white feathers, followed the girls. Hyacinth had never seen a chicken like Ramona Quimby. Sabine told her that it was a type of chicken called a Silkie, and Hyacinth wrote the name in her notebook to remember for when they were back home. Even though her birthday wasn't until February, she already knew she was going to ask for a chicken just like Ramona.

Sabine was convinced that her best thinking was done while sitting in her favorite tree, and when Hyacinth saw it, she had to agree. It was a Bur oak tree and must have been hundreds of years old. There were a few low-hanging branches they could climb and sit on—the perfect spot to hatch a plan.

"Okay," Sabine said when they had all scrambled up on the branches and settled in. She pulled off her backpack and opened it to reveal lots of goodies: a bag of perfectly beautiful peaches and a carton of strawberries, each as large as a golf ball. "What do we need to do?"

"I already told you: we need to stop Jessie and Orlando from submitting their applications," Laney said.

"But how?" Hyacinth said, biting into a peach.

"We could take their notebooks," Laney said. "The ones they've been scribbling in for the last couple of days. That's where they're writing all their notes."

Sabine tossed down a few apples for Chocolate Chip, Lady Lollipop, and Ramona. The animals rushed for the fruit, and the girls watched as poor Ramona tried to peck at an apple only to have it gobbled up by Lady Lollipop in one swallow.

"I don't know about taking their notebooks," Sabine said. "They'll probably remember what they want to say."

"Is the application on paper?" Hyacinth asked.

"I heard them say that they needed reception," Laney said.

"So that means," Sabine said, biting into a gigantic strawberry, "that they're probably submitting the applications using their phones. When is it due again?"

"Tomorrow," Laney said. "We need to figure out something fast."

"Well, it's pretty obvious what we have to do, then," Sabine said.

"What?" asked Laney and Hyacinth.

"We need to steal their phones."

# Ten

Jessie and Orlando worked on their applications all afternoon, taking a break only to head to a swimming hole with everyone in the afternoon. They read each other's responses, gave feedback, and rewrote portions over and over again. By the end of the day, Jessie's brain hurt.

They wandered into the kitchen, where Mama had finally been allowed to make a batch of jam thumbprint cookies filled with Sue's award-winning peach jam. Jessie and Orlando helped throw together a salad from the greens they had collected in the garden, while Aunt Amelia rolled out and cooked fresh pasta and tossed it with olive oil, cherry tomatoes, basil, and Parmesan.

After they cleaned up, they went outside and Aunt Amelia added wood to the fire pit behind their house. They gathered around the crackling fire, trading stories and looking up into the clear sky, where there seemed to be no limit to the number of stars.

✤ ✤ ✤

Jessie sat on an Adirondack chair next to the fire. On the log across from her were Hyacinth, Orlando, and Mr. B. Orlando was showing Hyacinth more chords on the guitar when Mr. B got a phone call and wandered off to take it. Mama, Papa, Uncle Sylvester, and Aunt Amelia soon headed into the house to go to bed.

"Who's Mr. B talking to?" Oliver wondered as they heard his laugh echo in the darkness. "He sounds happy."

Orlando looked up. "I think it's Aunt Penny."

"*Aunt Penny?*" exclaimed Isa, Jessie, Oliver, and Hyacinth.

"*Our* Aunt Penny?" asked Laney, incredulous.

Orlando grinned. "I saw her name come up on his caller ID."

Jessie smacked Orlando's shoulder. "How come

you didn't say anything?"

"I just did!" Orlando said.

"How long have they been talking?" Oliver asked.

"They spent a lot of time together last week, when she was in New York," Orlando said. "And I heard him talking to her in the van on Friday and yesterday."

"Wow," Isa said. "Aunt Penny."

"Does this mean she'll move to Harlem?" Laney said, jumping up.

"That," Oliver said as he poked at the fire with his marshmallow stick, "would be awesome."

Orlando shrugged as he strummed the guitar. "Who knows?"

Jessie squinted at Orlando. "Tell us how you really feel about Mr. B possibly dating our aunt."

"Aunt Penny is great," Orlando said. "And I want Mr. B to be happy."

"What can we do to help them get together?" Isa wondered out loud.

"No, no, no," Oliver said. "We're not getting involved."

"Why not?" Hyacinth asked.

"Because we'll mess it up," Oliver said. "Mr. B can

figure out his love life on his own."

"I agree," Orlando and Jessie said.

"Well, maybe we don't get *involved*," Isa said. "But we can help nudge them along—"

"No," Oliver, Orlando, and Jessie said.

"But if—" Isa tried again.

"No," Oliver, Orlando, and Jessie repeated.

"Oh, fine," Isa said. "But this is exciting stuff. Romance is in the air."

"Hey, look at the time!" Laney said abruptly. "I've got to get ready for bed!" She ran for the house.

"Us too!" Hyacinth and Sabine jumped up and dashed after Laney.

"Why do I get the feeling that they're up to something?" Jessie stared at their retreating figures.

"Voluntarily putting themselves to bed?" Isa said as she used a stick to push a log in the pit. The fire snapped and popped. "They're *definitely* up to something."

# Eleven

Laney slept in Sabine's room that night, telling Mama and Papa that she was joining Hyacinth and Sabine for a sleepover. Aunt Amelia set up a pile of soft blankets on the floor for Laney, and after the adults gave goodnight kisses, turned off the lights, and closed the door, the girls sat up and switched on their flashlights.

"What are we going to do once we get the phones?" Hyacinth asked.

"Hide them," Sabine said. "We could put them in the rafters of the chicken house. Or in Chocolate Chip's pen."

"We don't want the phones to be messed up," Laney said.

"How about hiding them in the van? We could

stick them in between the seats so it looks like they fell there by accident," Hyacinth said. "I don't think we're using the van tomorrow, and Jessie and Orlando won't look there. That way we won't forget the phones when we leave on Tuesday morning."

"That's a good idea!" Sabine said. "But can't you stay longer? Please?"

"I wish," Hyacinth said, "but we have to get to California. Grandpa really wanted Papa to go there."

Hyacinth and Sabine fell asleep not too much later, but Laney remained wide awake. The sounds of a farm were much different from the sounds of the city. Bugs buzzed and an owl screeched and coyotes yipped and barked. Laney knew all about these sounds because her first-grade teacher, Ms. Stone, liked playing the sounds of animals communicating with each other. Ms. Stone thought it was important for city people to be able to identify the sounds of nature.

The next thing Laney knew, Sabine's alarm was going off. It was three in the morning and time to grab Jessie's and Orlando's phones. After turning off the alarm, Laney tried to rouse Hyacinth and Sabine. But no matter how many times she shook them and whispered loudly in their ears, they would not wake up.

Laney sat back and considered what to do. She didn't like the idea of doing the mission on her own. Laney had such a fear of the dark that up until a year ago she would wake Hyacinth up when she had to go to the bathroom in the middle of the night. Now Laney wasn't as afraid, but the new place and the deep darkness of nighttime on the Harris farm made her uneasy.

Finally, Laney opened the door and peeked out. It was completely quiet and so dark that she could barely see a foot in front of her. She thought briefly about bringing the flashlight with her but decided it would only make it easier for her to get caught. New York City was always so bright with streetlights that she could always see where she was, even late at night. Here, Laney had to touch the wall next to her to make sure she was walking straight down the hall where Mr. Beiderman and Orlando were sleeping in one guest room and Jessie and Isa were sleeping in the second guest room with Mama and Papa.

Orlando's room was first, and Laney felt for the

doorknob. When she turned the handle, it opened with such a loud creak that she was certain they would wake up. She froze, waited for ten seconds, then peeked in. She couldn't see a thing. How would she find Orlando's phone?

She paused, hoping her eyes would adjust to the darkness. They didn't. Not wanting to feel around for the phone and accidentally wake Orlando or Mr. B, she was almost ready to give up and head back to Sabine's bedroom in defeat. Then she heard a faint snore. It sounded more like Orlando, so Laney cautiously moved in the direction of the sound, reaching out with her left big toe before taking a step. Her foot hit something solid, which she assumed was the bed. She put a hand out to feel around, and eventually her hand landed on what she thought was a bedside table. Finding the top of the table, she touched a book, then a water glass that she almost knocked over, then finally a thin object with a very smooth top. She picked it up, and the motion caused the phone to wake up and cast a dim glow. The photo on the screen was of Orlando and Jessie, so she knew it was the right one! Laney slipped it into her pajama pants pocket and carefully backtracked out of the room, closing the door behind her. It gave the same loud squeak, but again no one woke up.

In the flush of victory, Laney continued down the hallway to the other guest room, where Mama, Papa, Jessie, and Isa were sleeping. She could hear Papa snoring on the other side of the door. She was more familiar with this bedroom because she had slept there the night before. She knew that Jessie slept on the floor to the left of the door, so she opened the door and walked in that direction. But being too confident had a downfall, because she miscalculated where Jessie was sleeping, tripped over Jessie's foot, and crashed to the ground.

Papa popped out of bed. "Are the chickens okay?" he yelled.

Then Mama's voice: "Everything is okay, honey," she murmured. "Go back to sleep."

Laney kept still, trying not to even breathe. Eventually she heard Papa settle back down. A few minutes later, his heavy sleep breathing resumed. Only then did Laney let out a breath, grateful for two small miracles: one, Jessie did not wake up after Laney tripped on her, and two, Laney had fallen right onto Jessie's phone, which she picked up and pocketed as she stood.

There was only one task left, and it was the scariest one. She needed to go out to the van so she could hide the phones. Laney backtracked to Sabine's bedroom, only this time she veered right and felt carefully for the banister. Once she found it, she reached out a foot to feel for the edge of the top step and slowly made her way down to the ground floor. By the back door was an assortment of shoes. She couldn't see which ones were hers, so she slipped her feet into someone's too-large sneakers and let herself outside. A small light by the barn was on. Ludwig was parked not too far away.

As she shuffled toward the van, the heels of the sneakers scraping against the gravel driveway, she tried not to think about what could be hiding in the darkness. Tried not to imagine wolves or coyotes just waiting for a Laney-sized midnight snack. Pausing to shake a piece of gravel out of the sneaker, she heard a noise behind her. She spun around, but she couldn't see anything. She took a couple of steps toward the van, heard the noise again, and turned. Nothing was there.

Laney walked as quickly as she could in the large shoes and finally made it to the van. She slid open the door, went to the back seat where Jessie and Orlando usually sat, and slipped their phones into the crevice between two seat cushions. Then she scrambled out and closed the door. As she was about to rush back toward the house, she glimpsed what looked like a little white ghost standing right in front of her.

Laney *definitely* believed in ghosts, so she jumped back, slipped on the gravel, and fell to the ground. The little ghost made its way toward her, its movements jerky and awkward. Laney had always imagined that ghosts would move gracefully, floating on air, not teetering about. This ghost was not graceful, but before she could think too much about it, the ghost was upon her.

Laney threw her hands to her face and stifled a scream. The ghost stumbled into her bare arm, and it felt surprisingly . . . soft? Laney peeked at it from behind her hands. It wasn't a ghost after all.

It was Ramona the chicken!

Laney laughed as Ramona pecked around her. She must have gotten curious why a human was up at this hour. Laney stroked her soft feathers, then stood, brushed the dirt off her pajamas, and headed to the house with Ramona bobbing her head as she trotted next to her. Suddenly the night didn't seem so scary anymore. Ramona stayed with her until Laney was safely to the door.

"Thank you, Ramona," Laney said, giving her a kiss on the forehead.

Ramona twirled in a circle, then pecked her way back to the chicken house. Laney watched her squeeze through a loose board and disappear inside. Satisfied that Ramona was safely back home, Laney went upstairs to Sabine's bedroom, collapsed into her pile of blankets, and fell asleep.

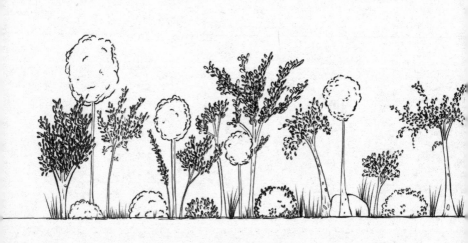

# MONDAY, AUGUST 11

Miles to Monterey: 2,226

# Twelve

Has anyone seen my phone?" Jessie asked at breakfast the next morning.

"I'm missing mine, too," Orlando said.

"That's weird," Papa said. "Is anyone else missing a phone?"

The adults and Isa shook their heads.

"I'll call your phones," Isa volunteered.

"I wish *I* had a phone," Oliver grumbled. "All my friends have one."

"Herman doesn't have a phone," Laney pointed out.

"Neither does Angie," Isa said. "Or Jimmy L."

"Everyone else does," Oliver said.

"I don't hear any ringing," Jessie said. "I might have put my phone on silent."

"I definitely had my ringer on," Orlando said.

Isa tried calling again while Jessie and Orlando left the table and wandered around the house, listening for their phones.

"Did you check the pockets of the pants you wore yesterday?" Sabine called after them. "That's where Dad always leaves his keys."

"Good idea!" Jessie said as she went up the stairs.

Oliver glanced over at his younger sisters. They were studying their breakfast plates with great concentration.

A few minutes later, Oliver watched Laney, Hyacinth, and Sabine leave through the back door and head for the chicken coop. Something was up. He crept out behind them, making as little noise as possible, then concealed himself on the other side of the chicken house.

"I can't believe you did it all by yourself," Hyacinth said. "You should have woken us up."

"I tried!" Laney said.

"Mom always says I sleep like the dead," Sabine admitted.

"It was okay," Laney was saying. "But the funniest thing happened when I was— Oh, hi, Oliver."

"What are you up to?" Oliver asked.

"Nothing!" the three girls said in unison.

Oliver narrowed his eyes. "What did you do to their phones?"

"Nothing!" the girls repeated.

"Yesterday you were talking about how upset you were about Jessie and Orlando applying for the scholarship, and now their phones are missing?"

"Oliver," Laney said. "Don't worry about it."

The door to the house opened and Isa stuck her head out. "Family meeting!" she called.

"Ooh, family meeting," Laney said, jumping up and dashing for the house. She was closely followed by Sabine and Hyacinth.

"I can go to your family meeting, right?" Sabine yelled. "I'm like family now, right?"

Oliver watched the girls run to the house. This was all very suspicious, but then he realized something important. If he didn't know what they were up to, he had plausible deniability when they got in trouble.

And Oliver was certain they would get in trouble. It was just a matter of time.

❋ ❋ ❋

The time at the Harris farm was so restorative that Isa dreaded being stuck in the van again. The only thing keeping her from setting up camp at the farm and never leaving was the thought of California. From everything she had read, California was beautiful. Even Mr. Van Hooten, who considered himself a lifelong New Yorker, loved California and had asked Isa to consider auditioning for the San Francisco Conservatory of Music for college. He thought she would love San Francisco.

The family meeting was all about the rest of the trip westward, which was a big logistical puzzle. The Vanderbeekers, Mr. B, and Orlando sprawled out across the Harrises' living room to talk. The space was not unlike their own brownstone living room, which was crowded with overstuffed couches and armchairs, the walls filled with bookshelves and cats lounging on every surface. The difference, however, was that the Harrises' living room was much bigger, with enough bookshelves to hold all their books without piling them up in corners or stacking them two deep. All along the southern wall was a row of big windows letting in sunshine. Tuxedo, Peaches, Cream, and Franz dozed on the turquoise carpet.

Uncle Sylvester was out in the field, doing something on his tractor, while Aunt Amelia sat in the kitchen with her computer. She was a writer for a big literary magazine and was typing madly away while at the same time warning Sabine to give the Vanderbeekers space to have their family meeting.

Papa smiled at everyone. "I still can't believe you're all here. This was the best birthday present ever."

"I love this place," Isa said as she petted Peaches.

"But not as much as New York City, right?" Laney interjected.

"It's funny," Isa said. "When I'm at home, I can't imagine living anywhere else. But then we drive across the country, and it's easy to imagine living on a farm."

"Don't even *think* about moving," Laney said, glowering at Isa.

"New York City is the best," Oliver agreed.

"Elberfeld rules!" Sabine called from the next room before she was shushed by her mom.

"Can we talk about the trip, please?" Jessie said. "I've been looking at Pop-Pop's itinerary. He wanted to see a lot of places, and I'm trying to figure out how we're going to have enough time to get all the way to California and back home before the end of the month."

"You could just stay here for the rest of the month!" Sabine called before she was shushed again and then sent outside to clean the chicken coop.

"It *would* be nice to stay longer," Isa said with a sigh from a soft couch.

"Hey!" Jessie said. "Let's stay focused. I've been doing some calculations this morning, and I mapped out a schedule."

"That will help when we're trying to find a place to sleep at night," Mama said.

"So we don't get into another Sady Cres Capround situation?" Oliver added, and everyone but Papa started laughing.

"What?" Papa said, looking around. "What did I miss?"

"We'll tell you later," Jessie promised. "Look at this itinerary first."

Someone's phone rang, and Jessie sighed. "Please put your phones on silent. It's really disruptive."

Mr. B pulled his phone out of his pocket, silenced it, then put it back into his pocket. "Sorry."

Isa, who was sitting next to Mr. B, noticed with interest that it was Aunt Penny who had just called.

Jessie took the map Pop-Pop had marked with the sites he had most wanted to see: St. Louis, Carlsbad Caverns, Albuquerque, and the Grand Canyon. Because her phone was still missing, Jessie had plugged those locations into Isa's phone and written out an itinerary. She put it on the coffee table so everyone could take a look.

"Based on my calculations," Jessie said, "we can get to Monterey in one week, meaning we'll have four full days in Monterey before we need to leave on Saturday, August twenty-third, to drive home."

"That's a lot of driving," Papa observed. He took a look at the original itinerary that Pop-Pop had put together, which Isa had encased in a clear piece of plastic for protection. "I can't believe my dad wanted to

Tuesday, August 12: Drive to St. Louis, Missouri (from Elberfeld: 2 hours, 38 minutes)

Wednesday, August 13: Drive to Wyandotte, Oklahoma (from St. Louis: 4 hours, 43 minutes)

Thursday, August 14: Drive to Lamesa, Texas (from Wyandotte: 8 hours, 37 minutes)

Friday, August 15: Drive to Carlsbad Caverns, New Mexico (from Lamesa: 2 hours, 40 minutes), then drive to Albuquerque, New Mexico (from Carlsbad Caverns: 4 hours, 46 minutes)

Saturday, August 16: Drive to Grand Canyon, Arizona (from Albuquerque: 6 hours)

Sunday, August 17: Drive to Barstow, California (from Grand Canyon: 6 hours)

Monday, August 18: Drive to Monterey, California (from Barstow: 6 hours) do a cross-country trip. This is so cool."

The Vanderbeekers looked at each other and grinned. Papa looked thrilled at their gift.

"Do you think we can do this whole trip and get back to Harlem by the time school starts?" Orlando asked, looking skeptically at the plan Jessie had laid out. "This only gives us a week to get home, meaning we would have to do about six or seven hours of driving a day. And that's not counting bathroom breaks, stopping for gas, getting food, and being sidetracked by flea markets."

"With Papa driving," Jessie pointed out, "each driver would only have to do about two or three hours a day. That's not so bad."

"It's bad when you think about sitting in the van for hours every day," Oliver said.

"At least we won't have Peaches and Cream by then," Jessie reasoned. "They'll be with Aunt Penny and you'll have more legroom."

"*If* she takes them," Mama pointed out.

"She'll totally take them," Laney said. "She loves them!"

"I don't know," Oliver said hesitantly. "She might

be too busy to take care of Peaches and Cream."

There was a brief pause. Then Laney pointed a finger at Oliver and exclaimed, "You want to keep them!"

"No," said Mama and Papa.

"I'm just saying," Oliver said, looking at the two cats, who were stretched out next to each other in the sun, "that if Aunt Penny doesn't want two cats—remember, we didn't ask her about them—we can bring Peaches and Cream back to stay with us."

"No," said Mama and Papa.

"If we follow this schedule," Jessie said loudly, bringing the conversation back to the itinerary, "we would have four full days in Monterey with Aunt Penny."

"Aunt Penny also said she would take us behind the scenes with the sea otters at the Monterey Bay Aquarium," Hyacinth said. "I can't wait."

"So we're back on the road tomorrow?" Isa said, looking wistfully out the window at the green pasture.

There was a chorus of affirmations.

Isa glanced at the itinerary, suddenly nervous about the coming days. They had never been away from home for so long, and it was strange to think that they were going all the way to the Pacific Ocean. She thought about George Washington, Paganini, and the chickens, about Benny and Allegra and Miss Josie, about her cozy practice spot in the basement and the bedroom she shared with Jessie. But then she thought about the adventures they had just had and the adventures ahead of them, and her homesickness vanished.

Wasn't it funny how you could feel so drawn to home and still feel an urge to explore the whole world?

* * *

Laney kept a close watch on her family that night at dinner. Things had felt like they were getting out of control earlier at the family meeting when Isa was talking about seeing herself living on a farm. A farm! But thankfully during dinner there was no talk of college or living outside of New York City, and Laney gave a tentative sigh of relief at bedtime when Jessie and Orlando still hadn't found their phones. Monday was now over, the application deadline had passed, and they could give up on the whole college-in-California thing.

Laney would never have to think about them moving away from New York City ever again.

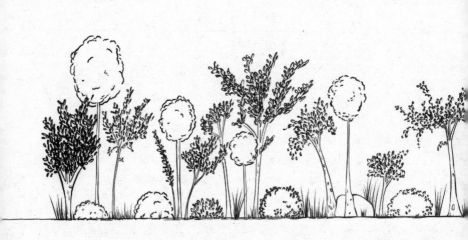

# TUESDAY, AUGUST 12

Miles to Monterey: 2,226

# Thirteen

The next morning, Hyacinth woke up in a dark room. It took her a second to remember that she was on the bottom bunk of Sabine's bed, many miles away from her own bunk bed in Harlem. She checked her watch: it was six o'clock, her usual wake-up time. Rain was hitting the roof with a steady thrum. She was used to the sounds of Miss Josie walking around upstairs in the brownstone, but not the sound of rain on the roof. She got up and peeked out the window, where she was greeted by gray skies and the occasional crack of thunder. The dark clouds rolled out before her like frothy waves, and she could actually see sheets of rain coming across the flat farmland, beating down on the earth. She leaned her elbows on the windowsill and stared out at the rain until she heard Sabine wake up.

"You're not *really* leaving today, are you?" Sabine asked, climbing down the ladder from the top bunk.

"I wish we could stay longer," Hyacinth said.

"Me too," Sabine said. "My parents said we can maybe visit you over Christmas."

The quiet of their morning was interrupted when alarm clocks began to go off and morning sounds awakened the farmhouse. It quickly got chaotic as people jostled for the bathroom, packed up their things, and ate a quick breakfast of fresh eggs and fruit.

It was good that Ludwig had been pulled into a spot in the barn the night before, because it was still pouring rain when they loaded up the van. Uncle Sylvester tracked down a spare tarp, which he helped drape over the cargo stored on top of the van, then secured the tarp with bungee cords.

The Vanderbeekers, Mr. B, and Orlando lugged their bags to the barn, and Papa jigsawed them into Ludwig's storage area. Peaches and Cream were found crouched under the guest beds—they didn't like thunder any more than Franz did—and were captured and put back in their crate. Tuxedo had no problem with the van or the thunder—he had been wrapped around Laney's neck, content to let her tote him around.

Jessie and Orlando still hadn't been able to locate their phones, even though they had searched every crevice of the guest bedrooms, their luggage, and their clothing. Hyacinth felt terrible watching them get increasingly frustrated. Finally, after an hour of fruitless searching, Mama announced that they had to get on the road. Aunt Amelia promised to mail the phones if they showed up.

With Papa joining them, it was going to be even more crowded inside the van. Oliver and Laney took seats in the first row, Mr. B squeezed into the second row with Hyacinth and Franz, while Orlando, Jessie, and Isa took the back row. Sabine stood outside the van in her yellow boots, downcast at their departure.

"We'll miss you!" everyone said to each other.

"Thanks so much for coming," Uncle Sylvester said to Papa, and they hugged before Papa climbed into the driver's seat.

Aunt Amelia blew kisses to everyone, and Sabine reminded Hyacinth to write her lots of postcards from the road.

Papa backed the van out of the barn and headed down the gravel path away from Harris Farm. Hyacinth looked behind her, and through the window she could see Sabine running after them, her boots sloshing mud. A minute later, Sabine stopped running and waved, and the van continued down the path and onto the main road.

"Do you want my map?" Mr. Beiderman called to Papa.

"We've got it plugged in to the GPS," Mama said from the front passenger seat. "Ugh, usually it's only a few hours to St. Louis, but there's major construction going on, so it's going to be more like four hours."

There were collective groans.

Then, from the back seat, Jessie cheered. "Hey, I found our phones!"

"Where were they?" Mama asked.

"Stuck in between the seats back here," Jessie said. "That's so weird. We haven't even been in the van since we got here."

"Yeah, so weird," Oliver said, glancing at his little sisters.

✦ ✦ ✦

The van turned onto the highway and everyone settled into their van activities. Hyacinth took out her guitar and rubbed the pads of her left fingers, which were sore from pressing down on the strings so much, before beginning her practice. Jessie put on her headphones to listen to a science podcast, while Isa put on her headphones to listen to a violin concerto she was currently working on. Laney used Mama's phone to call Grandpa to see how Paganini, George Washington, and the chickens were doing back at home and then began a friendship bracelet to send to Lucie, while Orlando helped Hyacinth learn a new chord. Oliver and Mr. Beiderman promptly fell asleep, and Mama and Papa talked softly in the front seats.

Farmland stretched before them as they left Indiana and entered Illinois. They stopped for gas along the highway and bought two loaves of fresh bread at a little bakery next door and ate it with Sue's jam. Another hour later, they saw signs for St. Louis and finally entered Missouri.

"How many states have we gone through so far?" Hyacinth asked, taking her notebook out so she could write them all down.

"New Jersey, Pennsylvania, Ohio, Kentucky, Indiana, and now Illinois," Jessie recited.

A few minutes later, Papa pulled up by the park that surrounded the Gateway Arch. The stainless-steel structure seemed to rise forever, its curved shape gorgeous against the clouds.

"The arch is as wide as it is tall," reported Jessie, who had been reading a guidebook that Aunt Amelia had given her about St. Louis. "And US presidents aren't allowed to go up in the Arch because it's a security risk."

"Wow," Laney said, craning her neck to look out the window.

"I didn't know you could go *inside* the Arch," Oliver said. "I want to do that!" He pulled open the van door and everyone got out and stretched their legs. It had stopped raining, but the sky was still heavy with clouds, and the ground was dotted with puddles. Franz happily sniffed the grass.

"I wonder why Pop-Pop wanted to visit St. Louis specifically," Isa said.

"I think my grandfather lived here for a little bit," Papa said. "I remember Pop-Pop telling me that he helped build a concert hall."

"Really?" Isa said, perking up. "Which one?"

Papa shook his head and pulled out his phone. "I can't remember. Let's see if I can figure it out."

After a little bit of searching, they decided that it must be Powell Hall, which housed the St. Louis Symphony Orchestra. The building was completed in 1925, which fit with the time Papa's grandfather might have lived there.

"I want to see it," Laney said.

Everyone else wanted to see it as well, so they decided to go that evening after dinner.

Because neither Mr. Beiderman or Hyacinth liked heights, they stayed back with the animals while everyone else went to go up in the Arch. While Hyacinth and Mr. B walked around the beautiful park, Mr. B got a call.

Mr. B groaned when he saw the caller ID. "It's Dennis, my new boss. I've got to take this."

While Franz sniffed around, examining this new world he had never visited before, Hyacinth listened in on Mr. B's conversation. It did not sound like a very fun talk. Mr. B was silent most of the time, occasionally saying things like "I will do my best to get that done by tomorrow, but as I mentioned before, I *am* on vacation," or "I understand, and I can get to it as soon as I return at the end of the month." Mr. B also rolled his eyes a few times, which Hyacinth had never seen him do before.

When Mr. B finally put his phone down, he sighed and rubbed his temples.

"Your new boss doesn't sound very nice," Hyacinth said as they sat down on a bench.

"He's . . . difficult," Mr. B said. "He's impatient to make changes in the department. I know I should give him a chance, but I miss my old boss."

"Did your old boss move to a different school? Maybe you can go work for him at his new job."

"I wish," Mr. B said, "but he retired after working at the university for forty-five years. Now all he wants to do is go on cruises with his wife. I think he's in Greece right now. I should probably check this email Dennis sent me. He needs me to review a grant application. It'll just take a few minutes and then we can get lunch."

As Mr. B squinted at his phone, Hyacinth petted

Franz and worried about Mr. B. She didn't like that his job was so stressful that he had to work during vacation.

Being an adult did not seem fun at all.

# Fourteen

When Orlando and the Vanderbeekers got back down from the Arch, they were pleased to find Hyacinth and Mr. B sitting outside on a tarp, a collection of picnic foods surrounding them. Clouds had dissipated, and rays of sunlight were breaking through and glinting against the Arch. Tuxedo, Peaches, and Cream were wearing harnesses attached to leashes. The cats looked happy, pouncing on the wet ground and chasing bugs.

"Tuxedo!" Laney exclaimed, running toward them.

"We passed a pet store on the way to get lunch and saw these cat harnesses. And we thought that if we're going all the way across the country, the cats need to be able to go outside safely," Hyacinth said.

"I'm so hungry," Oliver said, collapsing on the tarp and surveying the food with enthusiasm. There were grapes, sliced cheese, whole wheat crackers, carrots, a giant jar of peanut butter, berries, and hard-boiled eggs.

"This is perfect," Isa said, sitting down and grabbing a piece of cheese.

They all took seats, and for a few minutes all was quiet as everyone helped themselves to the food. A phone rang, and Mr. B sighed.

"Hi, Dennis," he said, standing up and walking away from the picnic.

"Who's Dennis?" Laney asked.

"Mr. B's new boss," Hyacinth and Orlando said.

"He also called half an hour ago," Hyacinth said.

"Really?" Orlando said. "I hope everything's okay."

Another phone rang; this time it was Aunt Penny on Mama's phone. She turned it to speaker.

"Hey!" Mama said. "We're all here!"

"Hi, Aunt Penny," said a chorus of voices.

Aunt Penny's voice came through the line. "How's the trip going? Did you get Derek?"

"We got there ten minutes before it wasn't his

birthday anymore, and he was *so* surprised!" Laney said.

Penny laughed, then asked if they were still set to arrive on Monday. She told them she had two guest bedrooms, plus a pullout couch in the living room.

"We're going to the aquarium, right?" Hyacinth asked.

"Of course! And there's a place not far from here we can kayak to where a colony of sea otters live."

After they hung up, Jessie looked at the map and planned out the rest of their day. Mr. Beiderman had found them a small rental house that allowed animals, so they cleaned up their picnic and headed for the van with Franz, Tuxedo, Peaches, and Cream in tow.

They drove a short way to the rental house. Since his boss had given him a mountain of work to do, Mr. Beiderman stayed behind with the animals while the Vanderbeekers and Orlando went to Forest Park, rented bikes for the afternoon, and explored the lakes, an amphitheater, and the World's Fair Pavilion. At the southeast corner of the park, they found the St. Louis Science Center and Planetarium, so they parked their bikes at the ride-share dock and explored the museum.

Jessie and Orlando had such a good time looking at all the exhibits, they agreed to leave only when a voice on the loudspeaker announced that the museum was closing for the day.

They ate Mexican food for dinner, then walked east toward Powell Hall. It was closed—no performance that night—but they admired the marquee illuminated with bulbs around the perimeter. While they were standing by the entrance, the sky darkening, the streetlamps turned on and lit the hall with a soft glow.

"Our great-grandfather helped build this," Isa said, pressing her palms on the brick building. The grooves felt rough and comforting.

"I wonder if he ever dreamed that his great-granddaughter would end up being a musician," Papa said, stepping next to her and touching the building as well.

"Maybe one day you'll play here," Jessie said.

"Or maybe you'll play with the New York Philharmonic and stay in New York City forever," Laney said, hugging Isa around the waist.

Isa laughed. "Either of those scenarios would be a dream."

Tired and happy, they walked back to the rental, where they found Mr. B asleep on the couch with the cats and Franz sprawled all around him. He woke up at their arrival, ate the dinner they had brought home for him, and listened to stories from their day. Then, while Isa practiced violin, everyone else got ready for bed.

Her family was asleep by the time she was done practicing. She changed into pajamas and thought about the events of the day. How amazing that they'd had the opportunity to see the city where their great-grandfather once lived! How surreal to see a building he helped to build! She climbed into the queen-sized bed where Jessie and Hyacinth were already asleep, images of playing in Powell Hall with the St. Louis Symphony Orchestra in her head as she drifted off to sleep.

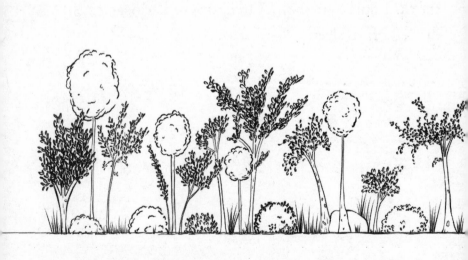

# WEDNESDAY, AUGUST 13

Miles to Monterey: 2,061

# Fifteen

The next morning, Laney woke up in a big bed next to her parents. Tuxedo was snoozing on Papa's chest, rising and falling with Papa's breathing. Laney thought about the past couple of days. She had been keeping a *very* close watch on Jessie and Orlando, and she'd heard no more talk about colleges or scholarship applications. She was confident that the phone stealing had been worth it.

Laney opened the door and slipped out of the bedroom. The other bedroom door was closed, so she assumed Jessie, Isa, and Hyacinth were still asleep. She walked to the living room, where Orlando was snoring, one leg hanging over the edge of the couch and the other draped over the top of the armrest. Mr. Beiderman, however, was awake, sitting on a stool by the kitchen counter, his laptop opened in front of him. He turned when he heard Laney come in.

"Good morning," Laney said.

"You're up early," Mr. Beiderman said. "I was expecting Hyacinth."

"I'm ready to start the day!" Laney declared. "What are you doing?"

"Work," he said, making a disgusted face.

"Still?" Laney asked. "I thought you did work yesterday."

"I did," Mr. Beiderman said. "My new boss is a nightmare."

Laney grabbed an apple from the fruit bowl and crunched on it while Mr. B hunched over his computer. Not too long after, her family and Orlando began to wake up, and the quiet of the tiny house transformed into a noisy collection of getting-ready-for-the-day sounds: Franz baying for food and the cats meowing and zooming from windowsill to windowsill to look at the birds. Papa and Oliver walked down the street to a bakery to buy bagels. Then they all packed up their things again and brought them to the van. Next door, a neighbor was watering her plants and waved when she saw them. She wore a huge floppy hat, over-alls, and clogs.

Oliver was the first one to get to Ludwig. He pulled the passenger-side door open and sprang back immediately, bumping right into Jessie, and they both toppled to the ground.

"What—" Isa began just as a feathered creature flew out of the van and into her face, its sharp claws scratching at her T-shirt and its wings smacking her head.

Jessie screamed, and Orlando got ready to grab it and tackle it to the ground.

"Don't hurt it!" Laney yelled when she saw the fluffy white feathers. "It's Ramona!"

The bird, recognizing Laney's voice, flew to her, landing gently on her shoulder and nuzzling the side of her head. Isa, stunned, brushed feathers out of her face and eyes.

"Who's Ramona?" Mama, Papa, and Mr. B asked at the same time.

"She's from Sabine's farm," Laney explained.

Mama raised her eyebrows. "Did you smuggle her?"

Laney shook her head as she smoothed Ramona's feathers with the tips of her fingers. "I promise I didn't. She must have climbed in when we were loading the van yesterday morning. Oh my gosh, has she been in there since yesterday? She must be starving!"

Oliver poked around inside Ludwig and came back out holding an egg. "Look! I found this under my seat on top of a blanket. She must have been sitting under there the whole time we were in the car. Also, there's bird poop *everywhere.*"

"Yuck," Jessie said.

"Of all the things," Mama said as she picked up the phone and dialed Aunt Amelia.

"Ramona must have been so scared," Laney said, comforting the bird. "Can someone get her something to eat?"

Orlando headed toward the house. "We still have some apples."

"You're bleeding," Jessie told Isa. "You're all scratched up."

Isa looked down, and her T-shirt was torn in multiple places.

Mr. Beiderman brought her the first-aid kit they kept in the van's glove compartment, and Isa cleaned her wounds and applied antibiotic cream while waiting for Mama to finish talking to Aunt Amelia.

"Here's the problem," Mama said when she hung up. "We could bring Ramona back, but it would be four hours of driving each way. We would lose almost a whole travel day if we bring her back."

"That sounds awful," Oliver said.

"But," Mama continued, "Aunt Amelia says that of all of her chickens, Ramona is the only one she's ever met that might do okay on a road trip. They raised her inside, and she really enjoys people. She said if Ramona has already bonded with Laney, it's unlikely that she'll fly away or wander off. Aunt Amelia said we can take her with us to California and then drop her back off at the farm on the way home."

"Really?" Laney said, her eyes lit up. "We can keep her?"

Mama nodded. "Not keep her. We'll drop her off

when we drive through Indiana on our way home."

"But she's going to poop all over the van!" Oliver said.

"I didn't even think about that," Mama said, then looked at her watch. "I really don't want to drive all the way back to the farm right now."

The neighbor who was watering plants next door turned off her hose and interrupted their conversation. "Why don't you use chicken diapers?" she asked.

Everyone swiveled toward the neighbor.

"What did you say?" Jessie asked.

"Diapers," the neighbor repeated. "For chickens."

"Seriously?" Oliver said skeptically.

"I used to keep chickens until the arthritis started acting up, and I made diapers for them when they needed to be in the house. You know, if one of the girls was sick and needed to be isolated from the others. I have a whole box of 'em if you want," she said.

"Really?" Hyacinth said.

Laney looked at Mama. "Can we?"

Mama shrugged. "Sure."

"I'll get them," the neighbor said, putting down her hose and heading toward her house.

"So the chicken will just . . . wear a diaper all the time?" Oliver said.

"I'm assuming we're going to have to change the diaper every few hours," Mama said.

"It's like having a baby again," Papa said.

"I'm definitely *not* changing a chicken diaper," Oliver said.

"I'll do it!" Laney and Hyacinth said at the same time.

Orlando came out of the house with some food scraps and sprinkled them on the ground. Ramona, famished, jumped off Laney's shoulder and pecked at the food.

A minute later, the neighbor reappeared, carrying a small shopping bag and pulling a wagon holding a crate. Papa rushed over to help.

"I thought you might like the crate for nighttime," she said. "That way your chicken can be free of the diaper for part of the day while it's resting at night."

Laney eyed the crate. Where would that fit in the van?

"That is so kind of you," Mama said.

Papa sighed and headed toward the van to see

where they could possibly fit another crate. He ended up wedging it between the two cat carriers.

"Great," Oliver muttered. "Even less space."

The neighbor showed them how to diaper Ramona. After the diaper was secured, everyone watched with anticipation for her reaction. Ramona seemed completely unperturbed, continuing to peck around in the grass. Confident that she was okay, they spent the next half hour scrubbing the van free of the chicken poop. Afterward, they loaded up the luggage, then got back in the van. After stopping for chicken feed and food for the campsite that night, they finally proceeded to get on the highway for the five-hour drive to their next stop.

They spent the late morning and afternoon driving across Missouri, stopping just after crossing the border to Oklahoma to head slightly north so they could say they had also been to Kansas. After calling Miss Josie to fill her in on stories from their travels, Laney leaned her head back and closed her eyes. Ramona sat in her lap, content to be on the road. Then Laney heard Jessie speak in a whisper.

"Oh my gosh. Check your email."

"Why?" Orlando whispered back.

"I just got an email from the scholarship commit-tee. Please tell me you got one too!"

Laney sat very still. If she turned around, they would stop talking.

"I got one too!" Orlando said, his voice happy and excited.

"Oh my gosh, oh my gosh, oh my gosh," Jessie said.

Laney could hear the springs of the seat behind her squeaking, as if Jessie was jumping up and down in her seat.

"I never thought we would get to the *interview stage*," Orlando said. "I mean, I can totally see why they chose *you*, but wow. Both of us. We'll be in Cal-ifornia on Wednesday, right? My interview is at two o'clock. When is yours?"

"Two-thirty," Jessie replied. "We need to figure out an excuse to go to UC Berkeley on Wednesday."

And then Jessie and Orlando stopped talking, prob-ably emailing Ms. Brown. Laney peeked around the van, but it didn't seem as if anyone else had overheard. Hyacinth was in the front row this time, absorbed in playing chords on her guitar. Oliver and Mr. B were asleep, and Isa was wearing headphones.

After all that work sneaking into their rooms and stealing their phones! How had her plan failed? Laney wasn't sure what to do next, but one thing was for sure: she was *not* going to let Jessie and Orlando go to that interview.

She needed another plan, and fast.

# Sixteen

Their campsite was just inside Oklahoma at a place called Gopher and Gazelle Campground. Hyacinth took the name as a good sign—she liked both gophers *and* gazelles—and when Ludwig Van rolled in, they were pleased to see no strange dolls staring at them from inside the registration cabin.

Papa checked in and got a map of the campground, and they drove to site number seven, Hyacinth's lucky number. The campsite was lovely, right by the Neosho River. Next to them, in campsite eight, was a family standing by the river, fishing. They looked up with interest at the Vanderbeekers' arrival.

Oliver opened the door, and the Vanderbeekers, Orlando, Franz, Ramona the chicken, and the three cats on leashes spilled out of the van. The kids from the river immediately abandoned their fishing and jogged toward them.

"Wow!" said one of the boys, who looked to be the same age as Orlando. "There are so many of you! Is that a chicken with a diaper on?" He leaned down to pet Franz, who was wagging his tail at 150 wpm.

Hyacinth hung back and watched the other family. There were three boys. The smallest had stayed by the river with his parents and looked a lot younger than Laney. She guessed he was four, and he was wearing a bright orange life jacket.

"I'm Bashir," said the first boy. He was as tall as Orlando and had dark hair and a big smile. "This is Hamad," he said, pointing to a boy who looked her age, "and Dawud is my youngest brother." He pointed back to the river, where his dad was carrying the little boy to meet the Vanderbeekers. "He's four and he's really tired and grumpy today."

Jessie introduced everyone while Laney removed Ramona's diaper so she could get some fresh air on her bum.

"We're here until Saturday," Bashir said. "How about you?"

"We're just staying for one night," Laney told him. "We're driving all the way across the country to California!" Then she told them about visiting their aunt in Monterey, and Hamad said they had gone to the Monterey Aquarium before and loved it.

"He didn't want to leave," Bashir said. "He wants to be a marine biologist when he grows up."

"Our Aunt Penny works at the aquarium," Laney said proudly.

"Wow," the kids said, impressed.

"And Hyacinth's favorite animal is the sea otter and we might see them in the ocean when we go kayaking," Laney added.

Hamad smiled at Hyacinth. "I love sea otters too!

They're so smart."

Bashir and Hamad's parents came over with Dawud and introduced themselves as Parveen (the mom) and Tariq (the dad). Their last name was Barsar. The Barsars helped the Vanderbeekers get their tents off the top of the van. Then, while the adults talked, everyone except Dawud, the four-year-old, ran to the river. Dawud stuck with his parents, sitting at their feet and drawing in the dirt with a stick. The cats roamed while Ramona pecked at a nearby patch of grass.

The Vanderbeeker and Barsar kids kicked off their shoes and waded in the shallow areas.

"You should stay longer than one night," Hamad said to the Vanderbeekers and Orlando. "Stay the week with us!"

"Yes, let's stay longer!" Laney said, thinking that it would keep Jessie and Orlando from getting to that interview.

Jessie shook her head. "We have 1,756 miles to go, and that's if we use a direct route without any stops or detours. We told Aunt Penny we would be there by August eighteenth. That's only five days away."

Laney grabbed a rock and threw it into the water.

"I think we should stay."

"Come on," Bashir said to Isa, Jessie, and Orlando. "Want to go swimming? There's a great rock for jumping."

The group split in two. The four older kids—Isa, Jessie, Orlando, and Bashir—walked along the river to a large outcrop. Oliver was going to join them, but Laney grabbed his hand and pulled him back.

"We need to talk," Laney said to him.

"Right now?" Oliver said, glancing longingly at the older kids.

"It's really important," Laney said.

"This isn't about the college thing again, is it?"

"What college thing?" Hamad asked.

Laney and Hyacinth quickly explained about Jessie's and Orlando's scholarship opportunity; then Laney updated them on what she had overheard earlier in the van.

"Wow, they *both* got interviews?" Hyacinth said. "That's so great . . . but also horrible." With this road trip, Hyacinth had gotten a new appreciation for just how large America was. If Jessie and Orlando went to California, how would she ever see them? Flights were expensive and bad for the environment. Driving would take way too long. The thought of Jessie and Orlando moving so far away gave her an immediate stomachache.

"I still don't see what the big deal is," Oliver said.

"If they get the scholarships, Isa will definitely want to go to California too," Laney said. "It will be the end of our family!"

Oliver shook his head. "They should go to any college they want to. Hey, are we done here?" He didn't wait for an answer before jogging off toward the rocks that Isa, Jessie, Orlando, and Bashir were now jumping off.

"I can't believe Oliver doesn't want to help us!" Laney said, watching as he joined the others. "He doesn't even care!"

"Bashir is looking at colleges too, but he wants to go to a school in Austin," Hamad said. "That's still in the same state, but I don't like thinking about him not living in our house with us."

"What can we do?" Laney said. "Their interviews are next Wednesday at two and two-thirty p.m."

"Why don't you tell your parents?" Hamad said.

"Maybe your parents can stop them."

"Our parents wouldn't stop them," Hyacinth said. "They would be one thousand percent supportive. So would Mr. B."

"I have an idea!" Laney said. "We're not supposed to get to Monterey until Monday, and their interviews are on Wednesday. If we get there late, they'll miss the interviews!"

They spent the next hour wading in the river and tossing balls to Franz while discussing ideas for stalling their arrival to California. It was hard to think of things that weren't dangerous or expensive. Hamad suggested putting something sharp under the tires so they would get a flat, but Hyacinth knew that replacing tires cost a lot of money. They thought about faking illnesses, faking injuries, and faking an emergency. All those choices seemed risky—if their parents found out, they would be in major trouble.

Laney wished Oliver would help. He always had such good ideas. All she could do was hope that something would just happen to delay them.

The older kids, done with their rock jumping, wandered back to the campsite. Jessie grabbed her shorts, and checking her phone, she noticed she had just missed a call from Aunt Penny.

When Jessie called her back, Aunt Penny answered right away.

"We're at a campsite in Oklahoma right now," Jessie said into the phone. "Yes, the plan is still to arrive on Monday."

Aunt Penny said something, and then Jessie said, "Wait, did you just say you're going on a *date?*"

Hyacinth, overhearing Jessie's conversation, sat up in interest.

"I mean, that's great," Jessie said. There was a pause. "Oh, he's a coworker? Wow, he sounds really nice if he brought you flowers today . . . What did you say? Hello? Hello?"

Jessie glanced at her phone. "I lost reception." She pocketed her phone and looked at everyone gathered around her. "Aunt Penny is going on a second date with some guy from work tomorrow. She sounds excited."

"I thought she was interested in Mr. B!" Isa said.

"I thought so too, but I guess the whole living-on-two-different-coasts makes it hard to start a relationship. This guy she's dating had a bouquet of ranunculus delivered to her office today."

"Oh, those are really pretty," Hyacinth said.

"I don't think Mr. B even knows what ranunculus are," Isa said.

"Mr. B is a million times better than that guy," Orlando said.

"We've got to get Mr. B to Monterey, quick," Isa said. "We can't just sit by and let some smart, thoughtful guy steal Aunt Penny's heart!"

"Hey, I thought we weren't getting involved," Orlando said.

Isa sighed. "I can't help myself. Wouldn't they just make the cutest couple?"

Jessie put her hands on Isa's shoulders. "Repeat after me: We. Are. Not. Getting. Involved."

# Seventeen

Jessie and Orlando set up the tents while everyone else played in the river and the adults built a fire at the Barsars' campsite and got dinner ready.

"I still can't believe we're both finalists," Jessie said to Orlando as they connected the supporting poles.

"Me neither," Orlando said. "And I'm especially glad because I think Mr. B is having work trouble."

"Work trouble?" Jessie said. "You don't think he's going to get fired, do you?"

"I don't know," Orlando said. "Mr. B mentioned to me that if his boss keeps acting like this, he might need to find another job."

Jessie knew how much Orlando worried about money and how he didn't want to burden Mr. B with college tuition. "So, how are we going to get to UC Berkeley for the interviews without telling them? I checked earlier, and the college is two hours from Monterey."

"Maybe we can tell them we really want to go to the Museum of Paleontology?" Orlando suggested. "That's on the UC Berkeley campus."

"And then we disappear for a couple of hours?"

Orlando considered. "Yeah, that would probably look suspicious."

"Should we just tell them we're finalists?" Jessie asked.

Orlando's response was immediate. "No." He paused, then said, "Sorry, I just don't want to tell anyone yet."

"That's fine," Jessie said. "We'll figure out a plan to get there." She pointed at the tent body. "Help me attach this to the poles."

"Are you nervous about the interview?" Orlando asked as they assembled the tent.

"No," Jessie said, surprised. "Are you?"

"Yes. I'm terrible at interviews. Remember last year?"

Unfortunately, Jessie did remember last year. The project they had worked on together had won first place in the district science fair, and a local online paper had asked to interview them. Jessie had come down with pneumonia after the fair, so Orlando had had to do the interview on his own. Not only did he talk so fast the interviewer didn't understand what he was saying, but he also attempted to be funny and came off as irreverent instead.

"You'll be great," Jessie said loyally.

"I don't think so," Orlando said. "I feel sick just thinking about it."

"We'll practice," Jessie said. "We can ask Ms. Brown to help us think about what types of questions we might be asked."

Papa called them for dinner, and Jessie and Orlando walked over to the Barsars' campsite, where Mrs. Barsar had laid colorful fabrics over the two picnic tables and set out five folding Adirondack chairs in different shades of blue around the campfire. On the table was a heaping pile of kebobs Mrs. Barsar had cooked on the grill while Mama had made a salad with toasted pita. There was fruit salad bursting with color that Mr. B had put together, and Papa set out a box of chocolate chip cookies the Vanderbeekers had picked up from a bakery in St. Louis.

It was as if the Vanderbeekers and the Barsars were meant to be friends. After dinner, they gathered around the campfire and swapped stories. Ramona Quimby made herself at home, enjoying the chicken feed that people scattered on the ground. Tuxedo discovered that he too liked chicken feed.

Dawud was so tired that he didn't want to eat, so Parveen got up to put him to bed in their tent. An hour later, Mama gathered Laney and Hyacinth so they could get ready for bed.

Jessie, Isa, and Oliver helped Mr. B and Papa clean up the dinner. Mr. B's phone rang and he wandered off to answer the call. Jessie wondered whether it was Aunt Penny.

"Did you know that Aunt Penny is going on a date tomorrow?" Jessie asked Papa. "A *second* date."

"She told Mama about him," Papa said. "I think his name is Harrison. I hope he's better than the last guy she dated."

"What was wrong with the last guy?"

"He still got an allowance from his parents even though he was in his forties."

"Does that mean I can still get an allowance from you when I'm that old?" Oliver asked.

"No," Papa said.

"Do you think this new guy is good enough for Aunt Penny?" Isa asked.

"Maybe we'll meet him when we go to Monterey," Papa said. "We can check him out."

"I already don't like him," Oliver said, frowning.

Papa laughed. "We should give him a chance, don't you think? I know Aunt Penny would like to settle down, get married, and have a family. Maybe Harrison is the guy."

Jessie looked at Isa. Her sister's eyebrows were creased in displeasure.

Later, when Jessie and Isa were bringing their bags of trash to the bear-proof dumpsters near the manager's office, Isa said, "If Harrison *is* the guy for Aunt Penny, then that means Mr. B *isn't*."

"We're not getting involved," Jessie said in a singsong voice. "Remember?"

＊ ＊ ＊

That night, hours after the food had been put away and the fire had been extinguished and Ramona Quimby had settled down in her cage and everyone was tucked into their tents and sleeping, Jessie woke to the sound of someone talking right outside their tent. She sat up and tried to look at her watch, but it was too dark. Then she noticed that Papa wasn't next to her, and she crawled to the entrance, unzipped the tent, and looked outside.

Papa and Mr. Barsar were outside, both looking at Papa's phone. The device illuminated their worried faces. Mrs. Barsar was sitting at the picnic table with Dawud in her lap. Dawud was crying.

"What's going on?" Jessie said.

"Dawud isn't feeling well," Papa said. "We think he needs to go to the emergency room."

"Oh no!" Jessie said, coming fully out of the tent. "Is there a hospital close by?"

"We're looking right now," Papa said. "We're having trouble with reception."

Jessie grabbed her phone from inside the tent

and saw that she had some service. She immediately searched for emergency rooms, quickly locating one about twenty-five minutes away.

"Here's one," Jessie said, passing her phone to Mr. Barsar.

"Thank you," Mr. Barsar said, copying the information into the notes area of his phone. Then he looked at Papa. "Are you sure we won't inconvenience you? I don't know how long this will take."

"You are not inconveniencing us at all," Papa said. "Don't worry. Keep us updated about Dawud."

"Thank you," Mr. Barsar said. "Either we'll be back before the kids wake up or I'll call in the morning."

Mr. Barsar picked up Dawud, and carried him to their minivan. Mrs. Barsar thanked Papa and Jessie three more times before getting into the car. A minute later, the taillights disappeared into the inky darkness.

"What happened?" Jessie asked Papa.

"Dawud has a fever and his stomach hurts even though he barely ate anything today," Papa told Jessie in a low voice. "He threw up a few times in the last hour."

Jessie used her phone to search the internet for

Dawud's symptoms. "Do you think it's appendicitis?"

"It might be," Papa said. "I told Tariq I would sleep outside their tents for the rest of the night so the kids will see me when they wake up."

"I'll sleep outside too," Jessie said.

Jessie and Papa went into their tent to grab their sleeping pads and pillows, careful not to disturb Mama and Hyacinth. Isa, Laney, and Oliver were in the other tent. They walked carefully to the neighboring campsite, using their flashlight apps to keep from tripping on rocks or roots, then settled their pads outside the Barsars' tents. The moon was out, but passing clouds occasionally obscured its light. Jessie looked up and sent a prayer into the universe for Dawud, staring into the eternal sky for a long time before she drifted off to sleep.

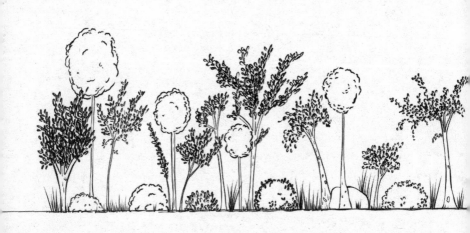

# Thursday, August 14

Miles to Monterey: 1,756

# Eighteen

Laney woke up the next morning ready to brainstorm new ways to delay their trip to California. She was surprised to find herself alone in the tent, and when she crawled out, she saw that everyone was clustered around the Barsars' campsite.

"What's going on?" Laney asked as she made her way over.

Bashir's eyes were glued to his phone, and Hamad looked nervously over his brother's shoulder.

"Dawud had a fever and wasn't feeling well last night, and his parents had to take him to the hospital," Jessie told her.

"Is he going to be okay?"

"They just called," Papa said. "He's scheduled for

an appendectomy this morning."

"What does that mean?" Laney asked, suddenly very, very afraid.

"His appendix is inflamed, and the doctors have to take it out or it could burst," Papa told her. "He'll probably have to stay in the hospital until tomorrow."

"And we're going to stay an extra day here," Isa told Laney. "So we can stay with Bashir and Hamad."

Laney felt like she was going to throw up. Just yesterday she had *wished* for an emergency to happen so they would stay on the road longer and Jessie and Orlando would miss their interviews, and now look what happened! Dawud was in the hospital, and it was all her fault.

"I'm so sorry," Laney blurted out before dashing into the woods, where a trail began. She ran and ran until she was out of breath and found herself back at the river but far away from their campsite. Sitting down on the rocks by the water, she was glad she couldn't see their tents. She didn't want to see anyone, especially the Barsars.

☼  ☼  ☼

The Vanderbeekers, Orlando, Mr. B, and the Barsars watched Laney flee the campsite and disappear into the woods.

"Did she just say she was sorry?" Papa asked. "What could she be sorry about?"

"Do you think she's okay?" Isa asked, looking worried. "She hasn't seemed herself lately."

"She's going to get lost," Jessie said. "She has a horrible sense of direction. Remember when she thought we were on our street and we were actually in Brooklyn?"

"I'll go after her," Oliver said.

"Me too," Hamad said. "I know where that path leads."

Oliver and Hamad set off along the path, which was lined with trees and grasses. They could hear the river but couldn't see it.

"Are you worried about your brother?" Oliver asked.

"Yes, but I think he'll be okay," Hamad said. "My best friend had appendicitis, and he had to take it easy for a couple of weeks after surgery, but after that he was fine. Bashir told me that it's really dangerous if your appendix bursts, but Dawud's didn't, so they just need to take it out."

It wasn't long before the path opened up and the river came back into view. And there, sitting on a rock with her head in her hands, was Laney.

"Leave me alone," Laney said when she heard them approach.

"We just want to make sure you're okay," Hamad said.

At the sound of his voice, Laney spun around.

"I'm really sorry," Laney said, her eyes red. "This is all my fault."

"What's your fault?" Hamad said, confused.

"Your brother being sick!"

There was a long pause.

"How is that your fault?" Oliver asked.

"You know how I've been trying to think of ways to keep Jessie and Orlando from going to the scholarship interviews, right?"

Oliver and Hamad nodded.

"Well, yesterday I was praying and praying for an emergency so we wouldn't be in California yet when they're supposed to have their interviews. And look what ended up happening! The universe listened to me, and Dawud got sick!"

"Oh, Laney," Oliver said.

"Dawud has had a stomachache for a couple days," Hamad said. "He's been so quiet the last few days because he hasn't been feeling well. Usually he's running all over the place. Him being sick has nothing to do with you."

Laney wiped her nose and looked at Hamad. "Really?"

"Really," said Hamad.

"Jessie told me that one in twenty Americans gets appendicitis," Oliver said. "It's really common."

"So it's *not* my fault?" Laney asked.

"No," Oliver said. "Although I'm impressed that you think the universe listens to you that much. Come on, let's go back to the campsite. Maybe there's an update about Dawud."

The three scrambled off the rocks and returned to the campsite. When they were spotted, everyone came running to make sure Laney was okay. As Laney was fussed over by Isa and Jessie, Oliver suddenly realized that his little sister had a very different relationship with their older sisters than he did. In a way, the twins had helped raise her. Laney would only be ten when they went off to college, younger than he was by two years.

And though causing an emergency to delay their arrival in Monterey wasn't the best idea, Oliver was pretty certain he could think of something that *would* keep Jessie and Orlando from making it to their interviews. After all, he wasn't a huge fan of them leaving, either. If Jessie and Isa ended up in California for college, he would be the oldest Vanderbeeker kid.

Oliver wasn't sure he could handle that responsibility, even if it *did* come with a bigger room.

✵ ✵ ✵

A little after one o'clock, Bashir got a phone call from Mr. Barsar.

"We're all so glad he's okay," Bashir said into the phone. When he hung up a few minutes later, he gave an update. "He was so tired that the nurse had a hard time waking him up to complete the post-surgery exam."

"Poor Dawud!" Hamad said.

"He's back in a regular hospital room in the pediatric wing," Bashir continued. "They'll monitor him today, and hopefully he'll be discharged tomorrow."

Their appetites restored by the good news, everyone finally ate lunch and then changed into bathing suits so they could swim in the river. Bashir got another message from his dad saying that Dawud was awake and happily basking in all the attention of the kind nursing staff.

Confident that Dawud was doing just fine, they went on a five-mile hike on a trail that began near the entrance to the campsite. It was just what they needed: strenuous enough to keep their bodies working hard; interesting, with rock scrambles that required them to think about where they were putting their feet; and plenty of beautiful vistas. When they got back to the campsite, they had more messages from Mr. Barsar, saying that Dawud was doing great and eating lots of vanilla pudding. They even got a few photos of Dawud with his nursing team, including one with a gigantic stuffed animal that looked nearly as big as he was. Then Mr. Barsar called and put Dawud on speaker so everyone could say hello.

After the call, they ate dinner by a fire on the Barsars' campsite. Orlando and Hyacinth took out their guitars while Isa played the violin, and Hamad dragged his cello out of his tent so he could join them. As the sky darkened and lightning bugs came out, the music kept the families company, along with the crackles from the fire, the rush of the river, and the hooting from a distant owl. Tired from the swimming and hiking, both families went to bed, only this time the Vanderbeekers dragged their sleeping mats out of their tents and over to the Barsars' campsite so they could all be together. They all spread their mats around the dwindling campfire, their exhausted bodies relaxing under the big sky, each of them thankful that Dawud was safe.

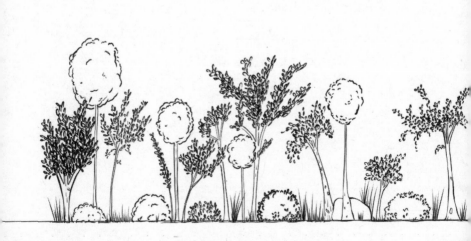

# Friday, August 15

Miles to Monterey: 1,756

# Nineteen

The next day, the Barsars and the Vanderbeekers woke to the best alarm anyone could wish for: the sound of the Barsar minivan's wheels crunching the gravel. Everyone jumped up and ran for the van. When the crunching stopped, Bashir yanked open the passenger door and there was Dawud, grinning and waving as if he had not just had emergency surgery the day before.

While Mama, Papa, and Mr. B prepared breakfast, Dawud showed them the big bandages covering his stitches and told them about his hospital gown with rainbows printed all over it and how one of his nurses gave him extra juice and how Mommy and Daddy had to sleep on chairs and now their necks were sore.

"I think," Mama told Mrs. Barsar, "that you should

take a nap, while Derek, Mr. B, and I take care of things around here."

Mrs. Barsar smiled but declined. They were going to head home to Dallas after breakfast, since Dawud needed to keep his wound extra clean and have a follow-up with his doctor in a couple of days.

"At least you're leaving today too," Hamad said. "It wouldn't be the same being here without you."

"We should go camping together next summer," Oliver suggested.

"Without the emergency surgery," Bashir added.

After breakfast, the families packed up their respective campsites, helping each other get the tents back onto the top of their cars and secured properly with bungee cords.

Then the Vanderbeekers were back in Ludwig and the Barsars were back in their minivan. Both vehicles headed out of the campground and stayed together for about half an hour before the minivan veered south toward Dallas while Ludwig continued on Interstate 44, weaving through Oklahoma and northwest Texas to get to New Mexico.

While Mama drove, Hyacinth and Orlando

strummed quietly on their guitars, and Ramona Quimby perched on the seat back next to them, listening to the music. Mr. B analyzed his paper map of Oklahoma and Texas, Papa fell asleep in the back row, Jessie read an old issue of *Science* magazine, and Isa listened to music on her headphones. Oliver stared out the window, while Laney wrote to Lucie using one of the postcards they had bought at the campground's registration office when they checked out that morning.

It was difficult for Laney to write about what she wanted to tell Lucie in such a small space, and as Ludwig Van rumbled through Oklahoma, she reflected on the poor design of postcards.

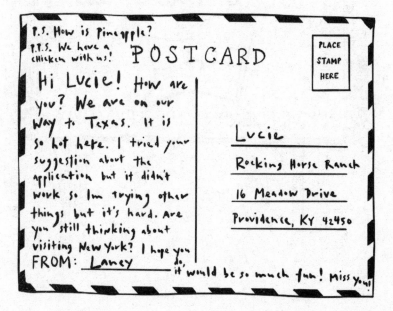

P.S. How is Pineapple?
P.P.S. We have a chicken with us!

POSTCARD

PLACE
STAMP
HERE

Hi Lucie! How are you? We are on our way to Texas. It is so hot here. I tried your suggestion about the application but it didn't work so Im trying other things but it's hard. Are you still thinking about visiting New York? I hope you
FROM: Laney do,
it would be so much fun! Miss you!

Lucie
Rocking Horse Ranch
16 Meadow Drive
Providence, KY 42450

They stopped after three hours to eat lunch at a taco truck in Oklahoma City, where Oliver ate seven tacos, his personal record, and Orlando ate nine, one short of his personal record. Hyacinth walked Franz and Ramona Quimby along the dusty road before they had to get back into the van. As they continued westward, trees slowly faded from the landscape and were replaced with tall grasses. They crossed the border into Texas, where they stopped at Wichita Falls to refuel and stretch before getting back on the road.

And because they still had many hours left of their scheduled driving for the day, they continued, even though no one wanted to get back into the van. Four hours later, they made it to Lamesa, Texas, their next campsite. They were all cranky and tired, and they immediately put up their tents. Everyone except Jessie fell asleep immediately. Once she was sure she was the only one awake, Jessie sat up and nudged Orlando.

"Blag," Orlando said when Jessie poked him in the ribs.

"Time to practice," Jessie whispered.

"Now?" Orlando groaned.

Jessie crawled out of the tent, and a few seconds later Orlando followed.

"The interview is next week," Jessie reminded him. "And no offense—"

"I hate it when people say no offense. It means the next thing they're going to say is going to be offensive."

Jessie ignored him. "You need a lot of practice."

As they made their way to the area by the camp office, Jessie let her mind linger on the scholarship opportunity. She couldn't believe they were in the *finals*. Everything sounded so perfect: spending next summer studying science at a major university with famous researchers and then getting to go to college for *free!* Her parents wouldn't have to pay a dime. Jessie would be on her way to achieving dreams she had had since she was in kindergarten, when her class went to the science museum. She remembered looking up at a wall with portraits of famous scientists: Maria Merian, who had studied the life cycle of the butterfly hundreds of years ago; Alice Ball, who revolutionized treatment for leprosy; and Rachel Carson, the famous environmentalist. Jessie felt a thrill just thinking about doing research that would one day make a difference in the world.

They arrived at the camp office, where one dim light illuminated a circle of benches.

"Okay, let's start," Jessie said, taking a seat on a bench and trying to look as if she were a wise and important scientist while at the same time swatting at a mosquito. "Tell me why you want to be a part of this program."

"For one," Orlando said, "I'm terrified I won't get into college, and even if by some miracle I *did* get into college, I would feel terrible asking Mr. B—that's my guardian—to pay for it. And I definitely can't ask my mom. I don't think she even has a job right now. Have you seen how much tuition costs these days? It's—"

Jessie cleared her throat. "Okay, uh, that's a good stopping place."

Orlando slumped against the bench. "I can't do this."

"No, um, that was . . . great. Maybe you should focus more on your aspirations and less on your . . . fears?"

"I shouldn't have applied for this scholarship," Orlando said, rubbing his head. "What was I thinking?"

"Orlando, listen. You're so smart and ambitious. You're a wonderful human being. What college wouldn't want you? Just be yourself and you'll ace the interview."

"I don't know about that."

"Come on, let's try again."

They went on for another half an hour, and Jessie would never say it to Orlando, but his answers seemed to be getting worse rather than better. Orlando, usually so self-assured and easy to talk to, seemed really uncomfortable talking about himself and his achievements.

Jessie finally discovered a downfall to Orlando's incredible humility: he was certain to bomb the interview.

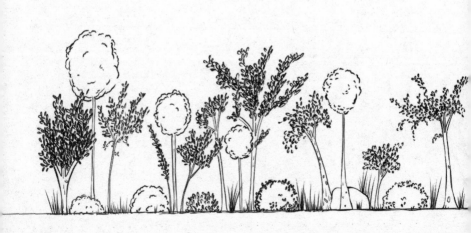

# Saturday, August 16

Miles to Monterey: 1,392

# Twenty

Hyacinth was getting tired of being on the road. She missed waking up in her own bed, having regular access to a washer and dryer, eating home-cooked food, and not having to be in the van for so many hours a day. On the other hand, she was getting a lot of practice on the guitar, and the pads of her left fingers were now callused over, so it didn't hurt as much for her fingers to be pressing down on the metal strings.

After breakfast, they packed up the campsite. They were getting faster and more efficient at loading up Ludwig. It was only an hour before they crossed the border to New Mexico, where they were going to visit Carlsbad Caverns National Park.

Mr. B had booked another cottage near the caverns,

knowing that pets weren't allowed in the national park. The rental was a little yellow house with a front door painted red. There was a cactus garden in the front, which Franz discovered when he accidentally stuck his nose in one of the plants. Hyacinth had to carefully remove the three spines with tweezers. There were two rooms on the main floor and three sets of bunk beds in the basement. They walked Franz, set up the litter box for Tuxedo, Peaches, and Cream, and settled Ramona in her crate.

Jessie had booked them a ranger tour at Carlsbad Caverns National Park, and as they got back into the

van, she looked up information about the caverns on her phone.

"There's a bat flight program in the evening," Jessie said.

Hyacinth shivered. She wasn't the biggest fan of bats.

"Speaking of the Eocene epoch—" Jessie said.

"Um, what's that?" Oliver interrupted.

Jessie sighed. "The Eocene epoch? The geological epoch that started about fifty-six million years ago and lasted for about twenty-two million years? Bats pop up in the fossil record around fifty million years ago, during that time period."

"I have no idea where this is going," Oliver said with a yawn.

"The point is," Jessie said, "I was wondering if we could go to the Museum of Paleontology while we're in California."

"The Museum of Paleontology?" Papa said from the driver's seat. "Where's that?"

"It's on the UC Berkeley campus," Orlando said.

"Berkeley!" Laney squeaked.

Hyacinth held her breath. This was about the *interview.*

"I'm pretty sure that's not close to Monterey," Mr. B said, leaning down to sift through his stack of maps.

"There's a top paleontologist who is giving a talk at the museum on Wednesday afternoon," said Jessie. "And Orlando and I are doing our summer science project on fossils."

Mama looked over her shoulder at the rest of her kids. "If it's that important, I guess we could do it."

"But we're supposed to spend time with Aunt Penny on Wednesday," Hyacinth said.

"I don't *want* to go to Berkeley," Oliver protested.

"Does that mean we need to be in the car for even *longer?*" Laney whined.

"Maybe anyone who doesn't want to go to the museum on Wednesday can stay in Monterey with Aunt Penny," Papa suggested.

"Works for me," Jessie said quickly.

"Me too," Orlando agreed.

Hyacinth couldn't think of a worthy objection. She

looked at Laney and Oliver, but they looked similarly out of ideas.

Papa parked Ludwig Van and they headed to the visitor center to see where they needed to meet their tour guide. They were directed to the basement where they located the ranger doing their tour. She was a woman with long black hair pulled into a braid that reached all the way down to her waist and she introduced herself as Pam.

While Pam was talking, Laney pulled Hyacinth and Oliver aside.

"They don't want to go to the Museum of Paleontology," Laney hissed. "This is for their *interviews*."

"We *know* that," Oliver said.

"Which means we need to figure out how to sabotage that museum trip!" Laney said.

Pam, the guide, cleared her throat.

Oliver, Hyacinth, and Laney looked up guiltily.

"I would appreciate everyone's full attention," Pam said. "We are, after all, descending to the deepest parts of the cavern open to the public, a full eight hundred and thirty feet beneath the desert surface."

"Wow," Jessie and Orlando whispered.

While Pam brought them down into the caverns and droned on and on about helictites, draperies, columns, and soda straws, Hyacinth thought more about how they could prevent Jessie and Orlando from getting to their interviews. Hyacinth had no idea what Pam was talking about, but Jessie and Orlando were quite absorbed in the tour and were always the ones to answer Pam's questions. Hyacinth could tell that Pam was very pleased with the interaction by the way she showered them with smiles.

It was an uphill climb to get out of the caverns, and when they emerged, they blinked in the late-afternoon light.

"I'm starving," Oliver announced.

They picked up dinner from a local restaurant, then went back to the cottage to eat outside on the covered porch. After dinner, Jessie and Orlando said they needed to work on their science project and headed into the house. Isa followed them to practice the violin, Mr. B took out his laptop to work, and their parents stayed outside on the porch enjoying the sunset.

Laney nudged Hyacinth and Oliver, and the three of them crept inside. Isa was getting her violin out in the living room, which meant that Jessie and Orlando must be downstairs in the basement. Quietly, they opened the basement door and inched down the steps until they could go no farther without being seen.

"These digital images of fossils are incredible," Orlando was saying.

"What's incredible is that they have the software for laser scanning, photogrammetry, and 3-D printing now," Jessie said.

"And if we can use X-rays to visualize fossilized biological soft tissue," Orlando said, "we can determine the copper distribution, and then maybe infer the original coloring of the feathers."

"We can definitely get more information when we go to the Museum of Paleontology," Jessie said.

Hyacinth looked at Laney and Orlando with wide eyes. Wasn't the Museum of Paleontology just an excuse to go to the UC Berkeley campus? Now it seemed as if they were serious about actually going to the museum. They listened for a little bit longer, but

Jessie and Orlando kept going on and on about *fossils.*

They went upstairs, leashed Franz, and told their parents that they were taking the animals for a walk. Franz led the way, and Tuxedo trotted behind as they went down the street.

"Maybe they're not doing the interview anymore?" Laney said hopefully. "I haven't heard them talking about it in a few days."

"But doesn't it seem suspicious that they want to go to UC Berkeley on the same afternoon as their interviews?" Oliver asked.

"It honestly sounds like they are studying fossils," Hyacinth said.

They puzzled over this new development all the way around the block. Even when they returned and got ready for bed, they were no closer to understanding what was going on with Jessie and Orlando.

✧ ✧ ✧

The Vanderbeekers and Orlando went downstairs to sleep on the bunk beds while Mama and Papa took one bedroom and Mr. B took the other. It was nice to sleep in a bed after many days of sleeping on the hard and rocky ground of a campsite.

Oliver woke up in the middle of the night, freezing cold. They hadn't been able to figure out how to adjust the central air-conditioning system, and one of the vents was blowing directly on him. His thin blanket was no match for it. He checked his watch. It was only twelve-thirty. He needed to find a heavier blanket if he was to get any sleep.

He went upstairs to see if there were any blankets in the hallway closet but paused when he heard voices from the living room down the hall. It was Jessie and Orlando. His footsteps on the carpeted hallway made no noise as he approached, and he stopped right before the living room to stay out of sight. He could hear Jessie talking.

"Okay, let's try again. Orlando, tell me why you're interested in the Berkeley program."

"I'm interested in this program for a number of reasons," Orlando said. "First of all, it was the college that Ms. Brown, my science teacher, attended. She spoke highly about it."

"Good, good," Jessie said.

"It's also the only program I really knew about, so I don't have anything to compare it to. I haven't done much research on colleges since I know a lot of them are really expensive—"

Jessie coughed.

"Ugh, I did that thing again."

"You started off pretty good," Jessie said.

Orlando sighed. "Does it feel weird that we're thinking about going to college a year early? Do you think we'll be ready?"

Oliver leaned his head closer to the living room. *What was Orlando talking about?*

"I know *I'm* ready," Jessie said. "I want to learn as much as I can as soon as possible. I can't wait to grow up and run my own experiments in a big lab."

"I want that too," Orlando said. "I just don't know if I can get there."

"You can do it," Jessie said. "I know you can. Let's practice again."

And Oliver, shocked at what he had just heard, slunk back through the hallway and down the stairs and crawled into bed. Two thoughts were swirling in his head.

The first was that Jessie and Orlando were very much still planning on going to the interviews.

The other was that they were planning on leaving for college even earlier than expected—a whole *year* early.

How was Oliver going to break the news to his sisters?

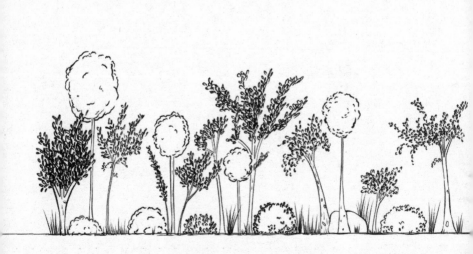

# SUNDAY, AUGUST 17

Miles to Monterey: 1,261

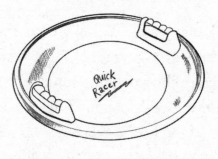

# Twenty-One

The next morning, Hyacinth noticed that Oliver was quieter than usual at breakfast. He didn't lunge for the pile of pastries that Mama had picked up from a local bakery. In fact, he didn't eat a thing, which Hyacinth could not recall ever happening, except for that one time when he had come down with pneumonia a couple of years ago.

Hyacinth needed to walk Franz, and she asked Oliver and Laney to come with her. Once they were halfway down the block, Hyacinth turned to her brother.

"Is everything okay?"

"I didn't sleep well last night," Oliver said. "I kept thinking about Jessie and Orlando."

"Why?" Laney said. "I don't even think they're doing the interviews anymore. They want to go to Berkeley to go to the fossil museum."

"Yeah," Oliver said, but his fingers were rubbing together, something he did when he was nervous.

"There's something you're not telling us," Hyacinth said.

"Yeah," Laney agreed. "Your fingers are doing that thing."

"What thing?" Oliver demanded.

Laney copied him.

"I don't do that," Oliver said.

"You're doing it right now!" Laney said, pointing.

"Okay, fine!" Oliver stopped and looked at his sisters. "I overheard them talking last night. They were preparing for the interviews. So that's still happening."

Hyacinth stopped and looked at her brother. His head was down and he was avoiding eye contact. They waited.

Oliver finally lifted his head. "Not only are they still preparing for the interviews, they're looking at going to college a year early."

Hyacinth and Laney immediately started to cry.

✧ ✧ ✧

Oliver didn't know what to do. His two younger sisters were bawling in the middle of the street. He was not equipped to handle this!

He stared out at the street, the girls wailing, his mind turning over the problem. They needed to make sure Jessie and Orlando missed the interview. And then the perfect idea came to him.

"Hey!" Oliver said, speaking loudly over his sisters' crying. "I have an idea!"

They looked at him, their eyes red and wet with tears.

"What we need to do," Oliver said, "is to make sure they miss their interview."

"We already tried that," Laney said.

"But instead of just making them miss it, we need to make them *think* that they *aren't* missing it."

"I don't understand," Hyacinth said, rubbing her nose with the back of her hand.

"We need to make them think the interview time and date has changed," Oliver explained, "so they show up at the wrong time."

"How?"

"We need to hack into Jessie's phone."

☙ ❦ ❧

Isa looked at her watch. They were supposed to check out of the cottage at eleven, and it was now ten-fifty-two. Where were Oliver, Hyacinth, and Laney?

The van was all packed, and Papa was doing one last sweep through the house. They did not want to recreate the Great Babo Disaster of three years ago, when Laney accidentally left Babo, her favorite stuffed animal, in a hotel and didn't realize it until they were halfway home. They'd had to go all the way back to Washington, DC, to retrieve it.

Isa walked down the driveway and looked up and down the street. And there, tiny specks in the distance, were her three siblings and Franz, heading back their way. She let out a sigh of relief.

"Where did you go?" Isa asked when they reached her. "I thought you were going on a quick walk.

You've been gone for an hour."

"We were exploring," Oliver said.

"We've got to get on the road," Isa said. "Come on!"

They piled into the van. Mr. B started up Ludwig and they were on the road, weaving through the beautiful desert. It was about three hours to White Sands, and Isa thought about the conversation she had had with Mr. Van Hooten earlier that morning. She'd had a virtual lesson with him, and he mentioned wanting her to visit the San Francisco Conservatory of Music if they were going to be in the area.

"Hey," Isa said as they headed west on US 82. "If we're already going to be near Berkeley on Wednesday, can we also make a stop in San Francisco? Mr. Van Hooten wants me to take a look at the San Francisco Conservatory of Music."

Laney yelped. "I thought you wanted to go to Juilliard!"

Mama, who was in the front passenger seat, glanced at Papa, who was sitting behind her in the first row. "Are we already thinking seriously about colleges?"

"It's only a couple of years before I start applying to conservatories," Isa said.

"Or even earlier," Oliver muttered under his breath.

"What?" Mama said.

"Nothing," Oliver said.

"So can we look at the campus?" Isa asked. "They have tours in the afternoon."

"I guess," Mama said. "Although I'm not emotionally prepared to be visiting colleges."

Hyacinth, who was practicing the guitar, strummed louder.

"Franz needs to go to the bathroom!" Laney announced.

Mr. B, who had an unfounded fear that Franz would one day have a poop accident in the van, pulled off at the next exit.

When the van stopped by the side of a quiet road, Isa watched as Hyacinth and Laney jumped out of the van, pulling Franz behind them. She thought she saw Laney rub her eyes, but since her back was turned to them, Isa couldn't tell for sure. When Laney returned, Isa forced Oliver to switch seats so Laney could sit next to her.

"Everything okay, Laney Bean?" Isa asked, looking at her sister's face closely. Something was definitely wrong.

"Yeah," Laney said, resting her feet on top of the cat carrier.

Isa put her arm around her littlest sister, and Laney curled up next to her and fell asleep.

Ludwig Van chugged faithfully down the highway. Isa was coming to love the beautiful desert landscape that was so different from New York City. As the miles went by, Isa almost wished they had more time on the road. There was so much of the country she wanted to see.

They stopped for lunch, and then, while waiting for the weather to cool down a little bit before heading to White Sands, they stopped by a building that housed local artisans, where Mama purchased gifts for people back home. Then they checked into another rental house and got the pets settled again. Finally, they drove to White Sands and parked, and Papa ducked quickly into the gift shop, returning with sleds and a block of wax.

"How are we going to use sleds here?" Laney asked.

"You'll see," Papa said as he started the van again. They drove to the Alkali Flat Trail, a path at the far end of the park. They set off, following orange trail markers.

The sand was white, Jessie told Laney, because of the mineral gypsum. It turned out that White Sands was the largest gypsum dune field in the world. When they reached a particularly steep dune, Papa made everyone pause. He pulled a sled out of his bag and rubbed wax along the bottom. Then he put the sled down, got in, and rocked himself forward, propelling himself over the edge of the dune. All of a sudden, he was careening down the slope, laughing all the way.

"Wow!" Laney said. "I want to try!"

Mama helped her get her sled ready, and off Laney went. They spent the next hour going up and down the dunes with their sleds, a much different experience from the times they sledded at St. Nicholas Park after a snowstorm. Watching Orlando squeeze into a tiny sled and speed down the hill—screaming—was something Isa was not going to forget as long as she lived.

Tired out, they settled down at the top of the dune and watched as the sky began to darken with the setting sun. The ripples in the sand combined with the dark shadows made Isa feel as if she were on a different planet. With each minute that went by, the sky and the white sand transformed from blue to orange to purple to pink. Finally, the last rays of light disappeared completely behind a far-off dune and the sky settled into shades of light and dark blues.

Isa looked at her family sprawled out on the dune, grateful for this time to be traveling the country with them.

Laney leaned her head on Isa's shoulder. "I love you, Isa," she said.

"Ditto," Isa said.

Isa felt very, very lucky indeed.

❖ ❖ ❖

The whole time they were at White Sands, Oliver had been thinking about how exactly to put his plan into effect. He was going to take Jessie's phone, find the email announcing the competition, and then create a fake email account and send a new email to Jessie and Orlando informing them of the revised interview date. When they went to bed that night, Oliver, Hyacinth, and Laney waited until everyone was asleep before they snuck into the living room, where Jessie and Isa were sleeping on the couches. Jessie's phone was on the coffee table, and it was almost too easy to grab.

Since Oliver was sharing a room with Orlando and Mr. B, and Hyacinth and Laney were sharing a room with Mama and Papa, the three shut themselves in the bathroom and huddled around the phone.

"Isn't there a password?" Hyacinth asked.

"I've known her password for years," Oliver said, punching in the code.

The phone made a short buzzing sound, but the home screen did not open. Instead, the password screen came back up again.

"How come it's not letting you in?" Laney asked.

"Let me try again," Oliver said, punching in the numbers once more.

The phone did the same thing.

"Did she change it?" Hyacinth asked.

"It's always been 'IsaV,'" Oliver said.

"Try 'LaneyV,'" Laney said.

Oliver tried it. It didn't work.

"Try 'HyacinthV,'" Hyacinth said.

That didn't work either.

"Try 'Laney' without the 'V' at the end," Laney said.

Oliver tried "Laney" and "Orlando," and then they got a message: "Phone is disabled."

"Oh no," Oliver said.

"Jessie is going to be so mad," Laney said. "She told me that if you try too many wrong passwords, the phone locks up forever and you have to pay the phone company a million dollars to open it up again."

"We are in so much trouble," Hyacinth said.

"Oliver, what are you going to do?" Laney said.

"Put it back where it was like nothing happened, of course," Oliver said. He opened the bathroom door to find Mr. B standing outside. He squinted at the light of the bathroom.

"I'm not even going to ask what you three are doing in there this late at night," he said, stepping aside to let them exit.

"It's not—" Oliver began.

"No," Mr. B said, putting up a hand. "I don't see

you." Then he went into the bathroom and shut the door.

Oliver replaced Jessie's phone on the coffee table, and he and his sisters went back to their bedrooms before Mr. B could see them.

If he couldn't get into Jessie's phone, how would they be able to go through with their new plan? And if they couldn't get the new plan to work, Jessie and Orlando would be one step closer to leaving them for California.

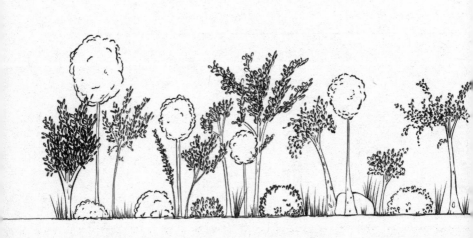

# MONDAY, AUGUST 18

Miles to Monterey: 1,136

# Twenty-Two

Laney woke up on Monday remembering their failed attempt to get into Jessie's phone the night before. Jessie was going to be so mad when she tried to open her phone only to discover it was permanently locked. Why did they try all those passwords?

Laney kept an eye on Jessie that morning, watching as she slipped her phone into the back pocket of her jeans. After breakfast, she noticed Jessie opening her phone. Laney held her breath and waited for the inevitable outburst. But Jessie seemed to be able to open her phone with no problem. What was going on? Laney was certain they had messed it up the night before, but now it seemed perfectly fine. She tried to pull Hyacinth and Oliver aside so they could talk, but there was no opportunity while cleaning up the rental house and packing Ludwig.

It would take a whole day of driving to get to the Grand Canyon, and Laney wasn't looking forward to being in the van for over eight hours. How were they going to find an opportunity to get Jessie's phone, hack into it, create an email account, and send an email changing the interview date? They needed to move quickly. In just two days, Jessie and Orlando would be heading to Berkeley.

The road to the Grand Canyon was a never-ending highway of rocks and canyons that were a totally new sight to the Vanderbeekers. Oliver sat next to Laney in the front row of the van, and behind them were Orlando, Jessie, and Isa. Settled in the last row were Hyacinth and Papa. Tired from the heat and the travel, everyone was dozing off except Mama, who was driving while listening to a true crime podcast, and Mr. B, who was in the front passenger seat banging away on his laptop. Laney could not believe how much work Mr. B had to do on his vacation.

Laney turned around to look at Jessie. Her sister's head was back, her mouth was open, and she was breathing deeply. Next to her, Orlando was slumped over in sleep, his chin on his chest. And there, in Jessie's relaxed palm, was her phone. Laney poked Oliver, who turned around.

"Get the phone," Laney whispered to Oliver.

Oliver turned and kneeled on his seat, then leaned over the back. Just as he was about to get the phone, Jessie coughed. Oliver and Laney swiftly turned around in their seats, pretending to stare out the window. A moment later, when all was quiet, Laney peeked over her shoulder. Jessie was asleep again. Oliver made a second attempt to get the phone. Laney watched as he lightly plucked it out of her hands as if he had been practicing that exact move for years. Then he spun back around and settled down next to Laney.

"Nice," she whispered.

Oliver had figured out the phone password situation when he borrowed Mama's phone and did a quick search. After six wrong passwords, the phone would shut down for one minute. After that, more wrong passcodes would lock the phone completely, and you'd need to be connected to a computer to get it working again.

Laney watched as Oliver tried "Mama," "Papa," "Maia," and "Derek." None of them worked. Then he put in "Arthur," Mr. B's first name, but the phone didn't open. He had only one more try before it locked up for good.

"You didn't try your name," Laney whispered.

"She would *never* use my name as her password," Oliver whispered back.

"Try it," Laney insisted.

Oliver shook his head but put his name in.

The phone opened.

There was no time to ponder why Jessie might have used Oliver's name for a password. Instead, Oliver quickly looked in her email, found the note from Berkeley, made a note of the administrator who had sent the original interview email, and read it. The email clearly stated that the scientist in charge of the program was very busy; no missed interviews would be made up. If that was true, their plan was perfect.

Oliver opened an internet browser to create a new email address using the name of the administrator. Once it was created, he crafted an email with the date and time change and copied the administrator's email signature at the end of the note. Then he sent the email to Jessie.

Behind them, Laney could hear movement. Jessie was waking up.

"Are you almost done?" Laney hissed.

Oliver didn't respond. He copied the email he'd just sent to Jessie, then edited it so it was addressed to Orlando, with an interview time half an hour before Jessie's.

"Why do I keep losing my phone?" Jessie muttered behind them.

Orlando woke up and shifted in his seat, helping her look for it.

Laney poked her brother, gesturing for him to hurry.

Oliver pressed send, turned the phone off, and reached down and slid it under his seat. Then Laney and Oliver sat back, their hearts pounding.

"Check on the floor," Orlando suggested, and they heard Jessie rummaging around.

"Found it!" she declared.

A moment later, Laney heard her whisper to Orlando.

A minute later, she heard Jessie ask Mama whether

they could go to Berkeley on Thursday instead. Apparently the paleontologist had a conflict and wasn't going to be there on Wednesday after all.

"That works a lot better," Mama said. "We're going to be driving so much over the next few days. It would be nice not to have to go all the way to Berkeley on Wednesday."

Laney looked at Oliver, and they shared a secret grin.

※ ※ ※

Orlando was freaking out. When they stopped for lunch at a roadside food truck, he pulled Jessie aside.

"I can't believe the interview date got changed," he told her.

"Isn't that a good thing?" Jessie asked. "It gives us an extra day to prepare."

"I don't want more time to prepare," Orlando said. "It's giving me more anxiety."

"You're getting so much better," Jessie said. "Just be yourself and don't forget what we practiced and remember not to speak out of fear and everything will be fine."

"Yeah, yeah," Orlando said, walking away from her and joining Mr. B at a picnic table. Mr. B was, as usual, tapping away on his computer, a grim expression on his face.

A moment later, Mr. B slammed his laptop shut.

"That's it!" he roared. "I can't take it anymore!"

A handful of food truck customers looked at him in alarm, and Jessie could see them considering whether they should create more distance between them.

"Can't take what?" Laney asked, running to Mr. B.

Mr. B picked up his computer and shoved it into his bag.

"Uh, Mr. B, maybe you should be more careful—" Orlando began.

"I'm quitting this job!" Mr. B shouted at the sky.

All talk stopped. A bird squawked in the distance. Finally, Orlando stepped up to Mr. B and put an arm around him. "It's okay, Mr. B. You did the best you could with your new boss."

"I can't even enjoy this vacation," Mr. B said. "Dennis is making me miserable."

A guy standing in line at the food truck called out, "Do what you need to do. You don't have to keep working for the man."

"Yeah," his partner agreed. "Follow your dreams and all that."

Mr. B looked at Orlando. "What do you think?"

"I don't think it's worth being at a job that makes you miserable," Orlando said.

"I'm going to submit my letter of resignation right now," Mr. B told him.

There were cheers around the food truck as Mr. B took out his laptop again. But when Jessie looked more closely at Orlando, she spotted worried creases on his forehead. Mr. B was now out of work, and Orlando's anxiety about getting the scholarship had just increased by a thousand percent.

※ ※ ※

After submitting his resignation, Mr. B was like a whole new person. He put his laptop away and vowed to not open it again until he returned to New York City.

"I've missed so many things on this once-in-a-lifetime road trip," Mr. B said. "Now I'm going to enjoy the rest of it."

Hyacinth noticed that everyone cheered except Orlando. Orlando had a smile on his face, but it wasn't the type of smile he usually had, the one that made his eyes sparkle.

"Everything okay?" she asked.

"Yep," Orlando said.

"Really?"

Orlando looked at Hyacinth. "Can I tell you a secret?"

Hyacinth nodded.

He lowered his voice. "I'm worried about money. Mom was always out of work when I was growing up, and I always felt bad when I needed something she couldn't afford. I don't want to be a burden to Mr. B."

"Mr. B doesn't think you're a burden," Hyacinth said.

"Yeah. I just know I'm expensive."

Hyacinth suspected he was thinking about college and not wanting to ask Mr. B to pay for it, and she was suddenly struck with guilt that they were jeopardizing his opportunity for a scholarship at an amazing school. Maybe she should tell Oliver and Laney not to change the date of the interview.

"Hey!" Jessie said from the van. "Time to get going! We've got four more hours of driving."

Orlando and Hyacinth groaned but headed back. Hyacinth chose a seat next to Laney and Oliver in the front row. Once the van was rolling and everyone was settled, Hyacinth leaned over and whispered to her siblings.

"I don't think we should send that email," she said. She went on to tell them about her conversation with Orlando. When she was done, Oliver and Laney looked at each other.

"What?" Hyacinth said.

"It's too late," Oliver said. "We sent it an hour ago."

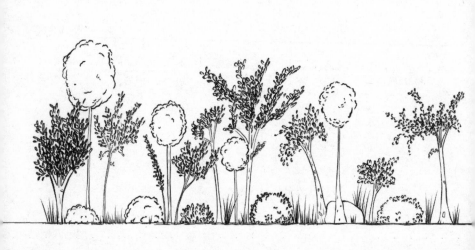

# Tuesday, August 19

Miles to Monterey: 731

# Twenty-Three

After all he had missed while working from the road, Mr. B was determined to make the most of the trip. He had downloaded a number of apps that would "enhance their travels." One was a map that showed various bizarre points of interest, which was why, on the way to the Grand Canyon the day before, they had ended up in a small town that had eleven enormous concrete dinosaur statues. Then, when they had arrived at their campsite and finished dinner, he had used an astronomy app to point out the various constellations, stars, and planets that were above them.

Mr. B had finally decided to embrace technology.

Tuesday was the last full day of their trip, and they were spending it at the Grand Canyon. Isa was puzzled at her siblings' strange moods. Jessie and Orlando appeared anxious, and her younger siblings seemed to be arguing about something but always stopped abruptly whenever she approached. She couldn't even get Laney to talk.

During a long visit to the Yavapai Museum of Geology, during which Mr. B and Papa insisted on reading every placard and then engaged in a lengthy discussion with a park ranger, Isa sidled up next to Mama.

"Should we be worried about them?" Isa said, gesturing to her siblings.

Jessie and Orlando were standing by a topographic relief map. Jessie's hands were on Orlando's shoulders, as if she was trying to calm him down. On the other side of the room, by the vintage photographs, were her three other siblings. They were sitting on a bench, staring out the window in front of them.

"I think they're just tired," Mama said. "We've been on the road a long time."

"Maybe," Isa said, unconvinced.

By that time, Papa and Mr. B were finally done talking to the ranger, so they left the museum and spent the rest of the day walking through the park. Afterward, they ate dinner at a restaurant, picked up the pets from the boarding place they had left them at for the day, then returned to the van. They had decided to drive through the night so they could get to Monterey by Wednesday morning. It was eight hours to Aunt Penny's house, and Mama, Papa, and Mr. B would take turns driving while everyone else slept in the van.

Even though she was exhausted from the hiking, Isa found it hard to fall asleep. All around, her siblings had conked out. Laney was next to her, her head on Isa's lap. Hyacinth, Papa, and Oliver were in the front row, Oliver propped up against the window and Hyacinth leaning against Papa. Behind her, Jessie was snoring and Orlando was muttering in his sleep.

The highway stretched before them in endless darkness, and the quiet of the van gave Isa plenty of time to think about the day. Her siblings had been acting so weird. She was certain something was going on. She had tried to text Benny about it but had gotten no answer; he was probably at work and not looking at his phone. It was unusual for her not to know what was going on with her siblings; somehow she felt as if she was missing something big.

What was it?

# WEDNESDAY, AUGUST 20

Miles to Monterey: 0

# Twenty-Four

It was nine in the morning, and the Vanderbeekers, Mr. B, and Orlando—all tired from the overnight drive from the Grand Canyon—stood at Aunt Penny's front door. They rang the doorbell, and after a minute Aunt Penny threw open the door, looking both thrilled to see them and completely frazzled. There was flour on her nose and flour in her hair, and there were flour

handprints on her black shorts. Franz jumped up and licked her face.

"Hi! I'm so glad you're here! I have bad news, but I hope you'll forgive me when you see the fantastic big breakfast I made for you all!"

As Aunt Penny ran around giving hugs, Oliver attempted to lug out the crate that held Peaches and Cream. The cats looked at him with so much trust, he felt an instant wave of guilt. He had been taking care of them for the last week and a half, and now he was just leaving them with someone who had never owned cats in her life. What were they thinking?

The guilt had become a common feeling in the last three days. A tiny seed of doubt had crept into Oliver's heart; he wasn't at all sure he should have sabotaged Jessie's and Orlando's interviews. He tried to talk to Laney about coming clean with them—especially after finding out that Mr. B had quit his job—but Laney had insisted that they could find scholarships closer to home. The plan wasn't preventing them from going to college, she said, just from going to a college *far away*. That was true, but Oliver still felt guilty. He couldn't shake it.

"What's the bad news?" Jessie said, squinting at Aunt Penny.

"Well," Aunt Penny said, fidgeting with her hair, "I have a work emergency and *might* need to leave this afternoon to go to San Luis Obispo for two days."

"What?" said Papa, Mama, Mr. B, Orlando, Isa, Jessie, Oliver, and Hyacinth.

"Where's Santa Luis Bisco?" Laney asked.

"San Luis Obispo is about four hours south of here. My colleague and I have a research paper that was accepted to a few conferences, and since I presented at a conference last month, my colleague Gabriela was supposed to present at one today and tomorrow, *and* we are supposed to accept an award for the work we're doing. But I just got a call that Gabriela's dad had a heart attack this morning. She obviously can't go now."

"Poor Gabriela's dad," Hyacinth said.

"I can't believe we just got here and you have to leave," Laney said.

"Well, I wouldn't have to leave until noon," Aunt Penny said. "After breakfast we can go to Point Lobos. I know you came all this way to see where your great-grandfather was stationed during World War Two."

"We also came all this way to see you," Oliver grumbled. "How am I supposed to teach you how to take care of Peaches and Cream?"

"Peaches and Cream?" Aunt Penny began. Then she caught sight of the cat carrier. "Oh my goodness, did you bring me the cats I loved from the bakery?"

"Surprise!" Jessie said. "We hope you're ready for a decade-long commitment to their health and well-being!"

"Make sure you brush them every day," Oliver said. "They like that a lot."

"Oliver is their favorite," Laney told Aunt Penny.

Penny leaned down and looked at the cats through the bars of the carrier. "My good- ness, they are even prettier than I remembered! I guess I'm a cat owner now? I have to buy cat supplies!"

The Vanderbeekers assured her that they had everything

she would need—Papa was already going back to the van to get the litter box, cans of cat food, and cat bowls, all items that had caused endless aggravation when he packed the car every day.

"Do you really think I'm ready for cats? Oh my gosh, is that a *chicken*?" Aunt Penny asked as she caught sight of Ramona hopping out of the van and giving her feathers a good shake. While Hyacinth explained why they had a diapered chicken with them, Aunt Penny ushered everyone through her house, passing a kitchen that looked as if a food bomb had gone off in it. Dirty pans and mixing bowls and wooden spoons covered every surface and overflowed from the sink.

"Ignore the kitchen, everything's fine!" Aunt Penny said as she led the way into the backyard, where a picnic table was covered with piles of food: towers of pancakes and bowls of fruit and baskets of muffins and hard-boiled eggs and several quiches.

"I love you, Aunt Penny," Oliver said as he gazed upon the spread, and immediately picked up a plate and started heaping food on it.

As everyone ate and updated Aunt Penny on all that had happened in the last week, there was a commotion at the side of the house. Franz barked at the gate, Ramona squawked and flapped her wings, and the cats—who were tethered to a tree—hissed and arched their backs.

"Penny?" a man's voice called. "Are you okay?"

Aunt Penny rushed to the side gate while Hyacinth grabbed Ramona and Isa grabbed Franz's collar.

"Harrison?" Aunt Penny said. "What are you doing here?"

"Who's Harrison?" Oliver asked.

"Aunt Penny's boyfriend," Jessie said, staring.

"She has a boyfriend?" Mr. B asked.

"She's gone on two dates with him," Laney announced.

"Maybe more," Isa said.

"I didn't know she was seeing anyone," Mr. B said. He squinted at Harrison.

Harrison and Aunt Penny walked over, followed by a barking Franz and a ruffled Ramona.

"I'm so surprised to see you here," Aunt Penny was saying to Harrison.

"You weren't at work, and when I called you didn't answer. I got worried, so I thought I would stop by,"

Harrison replied. "I didn't know you had company."

"This is my family. They came all the way from New York City in a van," Aunt Penny said, introducing everyone to him.

"I'm Penny's boyfriend," Harrison told them.

"You are?" Mr. Beiderman said. He looked at Aunt Penny.

Aunt Penny coughed. "We've been on two dates, Harrison. It seems a bit premature to say that we're boyfriend-girlfriend." She glanced at Isa, Jessie, and Orlando. "Do I sound like I'm in high school?"

"Yes," they said.

"Why are you dressed like that?" Laney asked, looking at his navy suit. "Are you going to a funeral?"

"No," Harrison said. "These are my work clothes."

"Wow," Laney said. "Do you work for the FBI?"

"Or a coroner's office?" Oliver asked.

"I work at the aquarium with Penny," he replied.

Oliver looked at Mr. B, who was looking at Aunt Penny, who was looking at the ground. Isa nudged Oliver's side and raised her eyebrows at him.

"Harrison, would you like to join us for breakfast?" Mama asked.

"Sure," Harrison said at the same time Aunt Penny said, "Actually, it's not a good time. My family just got here and . . ."

There was a long pause, then Harrison said, "Yes, of course. It was, uh, nice meeting all of you."

Aunt Penny walked him to his car while the Vanderbeekers watched Mr. B. The good mood he had carried with him since quitting his job was now deflated. The only sound in the backyard was birds chirping.

"So . . ." Oliver said, breaking the awkward silence. "Nice weather we're having."

There was no response.

"Sorry about that," Aunt Penny said, jogging back into the yard. "I had no idea he was coming over."

Oliver noticed that she avoided looking at Mr. B. Isa nudged Oliver again.

"Stop it," Oliver hissed.

"Are we done with breakfast?" Aunt Penny said, looking at her watch. "We should probably get going."

Everyone pitched in to bring the food back inside, pack up the leftovers, and load the dishwasher. When everything was clean and the pets were settled, they went to the driveway. Aunt Penny was going to leave for her conference right from Point Lobos, so she brought along a duffel bag and drove her own car. Mr. B, Laney, Oliver, and Hyacinth went with Aunt Penny, and everyone else went in the van.

"So," Aunt Penny said to Mr. B, who sat in the front passenger seat. "What's going on with work? Is your boss still terrible? I haven't talked to you for a few days."

Mr. B told her about his resignation.

To Oliver's great surprise, Aunt Penny said, "I have a friend who works at the Monterey Museum of Art and another friend who works in the art history department at UC Fresno. Have you ever thought about moving to California?"

✤ ✤ ✤

Laney could not believe it. Aunt Penny was trying to get Mr. B to live all the way across the country! It wasn't enough that Isa, Jessie, and Orlando wanted to go to college in California. Now it seemed that *every-one* was moving far away from her.

When they arrived at the parking lot for Point Lobos State Natural Reserve, Laney couldn't contain herself any longer. She jumped out of Aunt Penny's car and ran across the parking lot, nearly getting hit by a car that was backing out of a parking spot. The car honked and the driver stuck his head out the window and yelled, "Watch it, kid!"

"Laney!" Mr. B yelled.

"Laney!" Isa, Mama, and Papa yelled.

Laney could hear footsteps behind her, but she didn't stop. She veered onto a path leading from the parking lot and ran into the woods. A few minutes later, the path opened up and the Pacific Ocean came into view. Oliver and Aunt Penny were yelling her name, and it sounded as if they were catching up. They both played basketball and were good at running. Laney tried to get her legs to go faster, but her lungs were on fire. She felt someone grab the back of her shirt; then her foot caught on a tree root and she fell. Oliver tumbled next to her and they rolled downhill until they rammed into a fallen tree trunk.

"Laney!" Oliver yelled. "You've got to stop running off like this!"

The rest of her family, Mr. B, and Orlando caught up and surrounded her as she lay on the ground, her

T-shirt ripped, twigs in her hair, dirt on her knees and elbows.

"What on earth is going on?" Mama exclaimed, out of breath.

"You could have been hit by a car!" Papa said. "You know better than to run through a parking lot!"

Laney, filled with every emotion from the past week and a half, jumped to her feet and clenched her fists tight. "I'm so mad!" she shouted.

Jessie stepped toward her. "Why are you mad?"

Laney pointed at her. "I'm mad at *you!*"

"Me?" Jessie looked shocked.

"And you!" Laney pointed at Orlando. "And you!" Laney pointed at Isa. "And you and you!" Laney pointed at Mr. B and Aunt Penny.

"Why are you mad at us?" Isa said.

"I know all about UC Barkley!" Laney said to Jessie and Orlando. "I know about the scholarship application and how you want to graduate early and move to California and never come back!"

"Graduate early?" Papa said.

"Do you mean Berkeley?" Mr. B asked. "What's this about a scholarship?"

"And I know Mr. Van Hooten is trying to get you to go to San Francisco for music school," Laney said to Isa, "and that you're considering it! And now you"—Laney pointed to Aunt Penny—"are trying to steal Mr. B away from us by getting him to move to California!"

"You are?" Mama said to Aunt Penny.

"I—but—it was just a suggestion," Aunt Penny said. "Since he's looking for a job and I have some contacts here . . ."

"It's bad enough that Mr. Jeet is dead and gone forever! And now everyone else is trying to leave!" Laney said, sobbing. Her mind filled with images of an empty brownstone, all of her siblings and loved ones gone. No music coming from the basement, no thump from Oliver jumping off his loft bed, none of Jessie and Orlando's chatter as they worked out a science question, no humming from Hyacinth as she knitted. What would home be without the people she loved living in it?

"Honey," Mama said, putting her arms around her inconsolable youngest daughter.

"Laney," Isa said helplessly. "Why didn't you talk to me about all this?"

"I don't know," Laney said, weeping. "I never thought any of you wanted to leave until this road trip began. And now it seems like no one wants to stay at home."

"I wasn't even thinking of moving to California," Jessie said. "But this scholarship opportunity came up, and we applied because Ms. Brown suggested it. I never thought we would be in the final round."

Aunt Penny stepped forward and hugged Laney. "I'm so sorry. I never meant to hurt you. I want to say so much more, but I need to head to that work thing. I wasn't thinking when I said that about Mr. B moving here. Of course he's going to stay in New York City. I love you, and I'll call you from the road."

After Aunt Penny left, Mama turned to Laney. "I know change can be scary."

Laney nodded and wiped her nose. "Maybe we can all sign a contract saying we're always going to live at the brownstone."

"I don't know what the future holds for any of us," Isa said, pulling Laney into a hug. "I can't guarantee I'll live in the brownstone forever. But one thing is for certain: you are my sister, and I will always be there when you need me. That is a promise I will always keep."

Laney remembered what Sabine had said about sealing a promise back at the Harrises' farm, and she looked hard at Isa. "Can we spit swear on that?"

Isa raised an eyebrow. "Spit swear?"

"Sabine said it's binding forever," Laney said, spitting into her palm and holding it out to Isa.

Isa hesitated, then shrugged. "Oh, fine. This is how much I love you." She spat into her palm and they shook, and then Laney made everyone do the same thing, even Mr. B, who looked queasy at the thought. After the handshake, he vigorously wiped his hand on his pants, then used an unnecessarily large amount of sanitizer.

Once the laughter and exclamations of disgust had quieted, Mama looked at her kids. "We are family, and Papa and I will always love you no matter where you are."

"We will never be far away, because you live right here in our hearts," Papa said.

And in that place where she could hear the ocean crashing against the California coastline, where her great-grandfather had lived and served his country, Laney had an encouraging thought: Maybe distance was just a measurement. Maybe it didn't matter whether her family lived in different states or even opposite coasts. Maybe distance had nothing to do with how much she loved her family or how much they loved her.

Laney looked around at the people she loved most in the world and caught sight of Jessie and Orlando, and suddenly got that deep-down pit-of-doom feeling in her chest. She knew what she had to do. She swallowed, then said, "Um, Jessie and Orlando?"

"Yeah?" they said at the same time.

"I have to tell you something."

# Twenty-Five

Y ou *what?*" Jessie shrieked when she heard what Laney, Oliver, and Hyacinth had done.

Frantic, she looked at her watch. It was just after twelve.

"We might still make it," Papa said, pulling up the GPS on his phone.

"It's over two hours to the campus," Jessie said. "Orlando's interview is at two o'clock and mine is at two-thirty. Laney, I cannot believe you did this."

"It was Oliver's idea!" Laney said.

"Thanks a lot," Oliver muttered.

"It *was* brilliantly executed," Orlando admitted. "Jessie and I totally thought it was a real email."

"Why are we standing around talking? We need to

get on the road!" Mama said.

They raced back to the van and jumped in. Of the three adults, Mr. B was the fastest driver, so Orlando sat next to him in the passenger seat and gave him directions while everyone else climbed into the back and gave Mr. B unhelpful advice like "Go faster!" and "Can't you drive any faster?"

Before they knew it, two o'clock—the time of Orlando's interview—arrived and they were still ten minutes away from the campus. While they all anxiously watched the clock, Mr. B navigated the city streets as if he were a veteran New York City taxi driver and finally squealed into the parking lot. The lot was empty, probably because it was summer break, and Mr. B cut across the sea of empty parking spaces and slid right into a spot by the front entrance of the science building. Everyone tumbled out, and Jessie and Orlando dashed through the doors, ran up four flights of stairs, and located the correct department. A person who looked as if he was a college student himself was sitting at a big desk and glanced up at their noisy arrival.

"We're here for the interview with Dr. Bonavita," Jessie said, out of breath. "His appointment was at two o'clock. We're so sorry we're late."

The person glanced at the clock, then at Orlando. "Are you Orlando?"

Orlando nodded.

"I'm sorry, but it's two-twenty-two," the person said. "Your appointment time is past."

"Can Dr. Bonavita meet with him for even five minutes?" Jessie asked. "Or can he get a later appointment time? We can wait all day."

"No," he said. "Dr. Bonavita is booked solid with interviews. There are no opportunities to make up missed appointments."

By this time, the rest of the Vanderbeekers and Mr. B had arrived, huffing after the four flights of stairs.

"It was my fault they're late," Laney said when she got to the desk, practically collapsing on top of it.

"Actually, it was *my* fault," Oliver interjected. He was bent over, his hands on his knees as he tried to catch his breath. "I sent the email telling them that the day was changed to tomorrow."

"We did it because we don't want them to move all the way to California," Hyacinth added. "California is so far away from Harlem."

"But this scholarship is really important to them, so we told them what we did a couple of hours ago," Laney said.

"And we got in the van and came right away," Oliver finished.

The guy behind the desk looked at them with sympathy. "I'm sorry. There's nothing I can do."

Jessie stepped up to the desk. "I have the interview slot at two-thirty," Jessie said. "Can Orlando take my spot?"

There was a shocked silence.

"No, Jessie," Orlando said. "I can't do that."

"You can give him your appointment if you want," the guy said slowly. "But it would mean you wouldn't be considered for the scholarship."

"I'm *not* taking her spot," Orlando said.

"Yes, he is," Jessie said. "Please change the schedule."

"No," Orlando said. "I'm not doing it."

The guy looked back and forth between them.

"I'm absolutely not taking your spot," Orlando repeated. And then he turned around and walked away.

A door to the left opened, and a tall, gray-haired woman wearing slacks and an emerald green silk blouse stuck her head out. "Jessie Vanderbeeker? I'm ready for you."

Jessie looked behind her in case Orlando had magically returned, but he was gone. She looked at her family and Mr. B, who all gave her bright smiles and thumbs-ups. Then she stood up straight, took a deep breath, and walked toward the office and shook Dr. Bonavita's hand.

She stepped inside the office, and Dr. Bonavita closed the door behind them.

❋ ❋ ❋

While Jessie was doing the interview, Hyacinth went downstairs to search for Orlando. She found him in the lobby of the building, sitting on a bench by a statue of a man's head. Someone had placed a pair of safety goggles over the statue's eyes.

"How are you doing?" Hyacinth said.

"I'm fine," Orlando replied. "I would have bombed the interview anyway."

Hyacinth looked at Orlando's face. She couldn't

remember a time when he wasn't a part of her life, and in the past year in particular he had been like another older brother to her. She loved everything about Orlando: his kind heart, his big open smile, his laugh.

"I'm sorry we messed up your chance for the scholarship," Hyacinth said. "I feel terrible."

Orlando looked her, then pulled her into an unexpected hug.

Hyacinth's face was smooshed into his shoulder. "Are you okay?" she managed to ask.

Orlando pulled back to look at her. "In a weird, twisted way, it was one of the nicest things anyone has ever done for me."

"Really?"

"You and Laney and Oliver did all that because you didn't want us to move across the country," Orlando said. "To have someone go through all that trouble just to keep me around . . . Well, it feels pretty good."

The sound of footsteps caused them to look up. Jessie and the rest of the family were coming down the stairs.

Orlando stood up. "How did it go?"

"It's hard to know," Jessie said. "I'm really sorry

we didn't get here in time for your interview."

Orlando shrugged. "You know how I am with interviews."

"She was nice," Jessie said. "I think you would have liked her."

"It's okay," Orlando said. "I'm honestly very happy for you, and I hope you get the scholarship."

Jessie studied him. "Did you know that you're the best person in the world?"

Orlando shook his head, and Mr. B put an arm around his shoulders.

"Should we take a break and get some ice cream?" Mama said. "Aunt Penny told me about a fantastic place not too far from here."

The Vanderbeekers and Orlando looked at each other. Even though they hadn't talked about it, they had all been thinking the same thing since that morning when they'd seen Mr. B and Aunt Penny together.

"Maybe we can do something else?" Oliver, who had never declined an offer of ice cream in his life, said.

"Like what?" Papa asked, his eyebrow raised.

"How about a trip to San Luis Obispo?" Isa asked.

# Twenty-Six

Mr. B's head shot up at the suggestion that they go to San Luis Obispo.

"C'mon, Mr. B," Isa said. "We tried to stay out of your love life, but it's time for you to step up. We know you like Aunt Penny."

"You *like-like* her," Laney added.

"She's got a boyfriend," Mr. B said.

"She didn't seem too excited about him this morning," Oliver said.

"If you really like her," Hyacinth said, "you need to do a grand gesture."

"Grand gestures always work in the movies," Orlando agreed.

Mr. B looked at Mama and Papa. "What do you think about this?"

"There's no one better than Penny," Mama said.

"Go for it, Arthur," Papa said. "Chase your happiness."

They all looked at Mr. B expectantly, waiting for his response.

Just as Hyacinth was about to give up on him, Mr. B stood up tall and raised his arms above his head. "Let's do it. Let's go to San Luis Obispo."

It appeared that their road trip was not quite over.

✵ ✵ ✵

When the Vanderbeekers, Mr. B, and Orlando got back into the van, Jessie insisted that they stop by a clothing store.

"Is this really the time to shop for clothes?" Oliver asked her. "Mr. B's love life is on the line!"

"It's clothes *for* Mr. B!" Jessie said.

"What's wrong with my clothes?" Mr. B asked.

"Trust me, you'll want a new shirt at least," Jessie said, looking at Mr. B's "uniform" of a black shirt and black pants and black socks.

"The grand gesture," Orlando said, and everyone else nodded.

Mr. B reluctantly agreed, and Papa stopped the van on a street with a number of clothing shops. Orlando selected a store that looked as if it might have dressy shirts, and they went inside. A very energetic man greeted them.

"Welcome to Jupiter's Closet!" the guy said. "I'm Freddy. Can I help you with anything?" Freddy caught sight of Mr. B's fluorescent yellow shoes. "Ooh, I love your shoes. Great color."

"We need an outfit for him," Jessie said, pushing Mr. B in front of the group.

"Are you shopping for an event?" Freddy asked. "Or hiking? A dinner party, maybe? Are you looking for an outfit for a relaxed Sunday, or a business Monday?"

"He needs to make a good impression on our aunt," Oliver told him.

"He *like-likes* her!" Laney said.

"Excellent," Freddy said. He walked briskly toward the men's section, everyone jogging to keep up with him. Freddy flipped through the hangers with a crisp efficiency. "So you're telling me he needs to make an impact. I saw something this morning that caught my eye . . . Oh, here it is!" He yanked out a silky purple shirt.

Mr. Beiderman squinted. "Are you sure? It looks very . . . purple. And small."

"You look great in purple," Laney said. "Remember that shirt I made for you for the marathon? Hey, how come you don't wear that anymore?"

"It's supposed to be fitted," Freddy assured him. "Unfortunately, I don't have another purple shirt in the next size in stock right now. Why don't you try it on and see what you think?"

"We don't have time to try it on!" Jessie said, swiping the shirt from him. She pushed it into Mr. B's hands. "It's perfect. You can change into this right before we see her. I don't want you to get it wrinkled on the car ride."

Mr. B handed over his credit card and paid for the shirt. They all thanked Freddy and headed back to the van. On the way, they came upon a florist that had buckets of flowers in every shade of purple, pink, yellow, and orange.

"You have to get her a bouquet," Isa said. "She likes flowers."

When Mr. B hesitated, Orlando said, "Grand gesture, remember!"

"Fine," Mr. B grumbled, and they filed into the tiny shop.

"He needs a huge, beautiful bouquet for the woman he's trying to win over," Isa told the shop owner.

"Something *very* expensive," Jessie added. "It needs to make an impact."

The woman clasped her hands in delight, then scurried outside to gather armfuls of ranunculus, plumosa ferns, peonies, and garden roses. She wrapped the blooms in delicate tissue but bound the bottom of the stems in wet paper towels to keep them fresh. She tied three ivory ribbons of varying widths around everything and set the bouquet on the counter.

Once again, Mr. B handed over his credit card ("This grand-gesture thing is costing a lot of money," he said), and they ran back to the van. Papa turned Ludwig Van south toward San Luis Obispo while Jessie tried to look up conferences that Aunt Penny could be at. After a lot of scrolling, she found that the International Conference on Coastal Health and Marine Ecosystems was being held at a convention center in the area.

It was a four-hour drive from Berkeley to San Luis Obispo, an eternity away. An hour into the trip, Hyacinth, who was strumming her guitar, paused her playing and looked thoughtfully at Mr. B.

"What are you going to say when you see Aunt Penny?" she asked.

"Um," Mr. B said. "I'm going to tell her that I hope she's not really dating that Harrison guy?"

"Okay, and then what?"

"And then I'll . . . give her the flowers?"

"And then?"

"And then . . ." Mr. Beiderman ran a hand through his hair in frustration. "I don't know. I'm not good in these situations!"

Hyacinth patted Mr. B's shoulder. "Don't worry. You'll know the perfect thing to say once you see her."

It was nearly eight o'clock when they arrived in San Luis Obispo. Mama knew that Aunt Penny was at a fancy dinner because she had gotten a text from her. Aunt Penny had sent a picture of herself all dressed up.

Mr. Beiderman saw the photo and said, "Wow."

The Vanderbeeker kids saw the photo and Jessie said, "See? Aren't you glad I made you buy a new shirt?"

When they were five minutes away from the convention center, Mr. B changed from his black T-shirt into the purple silk shirt.

"This is too small," Mr. B said. He had to suck a breath in to button it up.

Jessie looked at him. It *was* a little too small, but she wasn't going to admit that. She regretted not letting him try it on. "It looks great."

Papa pulled into a circular driveway right in front of the convention center. A huge banner that said ICCHME: INTERNATIONAL CONFERENCE ON COASTAL HEALTH AND MARINE ECOSYSTEMS: THE FUTURE OF OUR OCEANS stretched above the doors.

Jessie glanced at Mr. B in his too-small purple silk shirt and the bouquet of flowers gripped so tightly in his hands that his knuckles had turned white.

It was time to find Aunt Penny.

# Twenty-Seven

Mr. B, the Vanderbeeker kids, and Orlando tumbled out of the van. They left Franz, Tuxedo, and Ramona Quimby in the van with Mama and Papa. On the sidewalk in front of the convention center, Mr. B was looking down at his shirt. The buttons strained against the fabric as he breathed.

"This shirt isn't working," Mr. B said. "It's too small."

"I think it looks fine," Hyacinth fibbed, biting her lip. Mr. B had been keeping in shape by running with Orlando in the past year and a half, but the week of sitting in the van, eating on the road, and not getting much exercise was catching up to him.

"Maybe I should change back into my normal

shirt," Mr. B said, turning toward the van.

"No time to change," Jessie said, pulling him toward the entrance.

They went through the doors and stepped inside the cavernous convention center. There were staircases and elevators in every direction, and huge screens advertised various sessions. Across the giant lobby area was a large set of closed doors. Above the doors were the words "Reception: Banquet Hall A."

"Hey!" said someone as they raced by the registration desk. "You can't be here without a badge!"

"Are those animals?" said a person at the information table. "No pets allowed! Hey, stop!"

Hyacinth looked behind her, and Franz and Tuxedo were galloping after them, with Ramona Quimby pulling up the rear, her wings spread as she scurried to keep up.

"How did they get out?" Jessie yelled.

"You were the last one out of the van," Isa yelled back. "Didn't you close the door?"

Jessie's eyes widened. "I thought Orlando closed it!"

"I was helping Mr. B with the flowers. I thought

*you* closed it!" Orlando yelled back.

But it was too late to stop now. If they did, they would never be let back in. Franz caught up to Hyacinth, and she grabbed the leash that was dragging behind him. Laney scooped up Tuxedo, and Ramona jumped and landed on Hyacinth's shoulder.

When Oliver got to the banquet hall doors, he flung them open. The room was dimly lit, and people were standing at tall circular tables with wineglasses in their hands, their attention on the podium at the opposite side of the room. And to their surprise, behind the podium was Aunt Penny.

"Our continuing research is allowing us to further examine why sea otter repopulation efforts have stalled while also exploring possible best practices for species reintroduction," Aunt Penny was saying.

But more and more people were turning their attention from Aunt Penny to look at the Vanderbeekers, Mr. B, and Orlando. Franz lunged for the dessert sitting on a side table, nearly pulling Hyacinth to the ground.

"Franz, stop!" Hyacinth hissed, not wanting to interrupt Aunt Penny's speech. Ramona, startled, flapped her wings. Feathers flew in every direction, including onto the dessert dishes of nearby diners.

Mr. Beiderman was oblivious to the commotion they were causing. His eyes were only on Aunt Penny.

"It is always a privilege to present our findings, and our team is so grateful for this award—" Aunt Penny said.

"BOK!" cried Ramona. "BOK BOK SQUAWK!"

"RUFF!" woofed Franz. "ARRR-OOOOO!"

Aunt Penny paused and peered out at the audience. She leaned forward and squinted. "Arthur? Isa? Is everything okay?"

Mr. B, Orlando, and the Vanderbeekers, knowing that they had already interrupted everything, had no choice but to make their way to the podium. Franz sprang for a piece of cake on a nearby table.

"Penny!" Mr. B said as he arrived in front of her, the flowers gripped tightly in his hand, his yellow shoes glowing in the overhead light shining on the podium.

Aunt Penny looked down on him, her face panicked. "What's going on?"

Mr. B was breathing so hard that two buttons popped off his purple silk shirt and fell to the ground, quickly becoming one with the carpet's brown and orange swirls.

Orlando nudged Mr. B forward. Mr. B stumbled as he went up the three steps to the podium.

"The flowers!" Hyacinth whispered loudly.

Mr. B held the flowers out to her. "Everything's fine. I brought these for you."

"Uh, thank you?" Aunt Penny said.

Mr. B looked around him. Everyone was staring at him. "I'm so sorry we interrupted your event," he said to the audience. "I've never done anything like this before, but since we've already created such a disturbance, I wonder if you wouldn't mind if I quickly tell Penny something before I lose my nerve? It will only take a minute."

There were affirmative murmurs and nods from the audience, as well as a couple of wolf whistles.

Mr. B turned back to Aunt Penny. He took a deep breath and stared into her eyes. "I think you're so smart and beautiful, and I never get tired of talking to you. The best part of my day is when my phone rings and your name is on the caller ID. I think about you all the time, wondering what you're doing, what you're eating, what's putting a smile on your face. I know you're seeing someone else right now, and I know I live across the country in New York City and you live in Monterey, but I had to say something before any more time passed. I'm probably too late, but I couldn't go another minute without telling you how I feel. I'm in love with you, Penny."

Mr. B was breathing hard, as if he had just finished running a marathon. Conversely, the reception hall was completely still. No one moved a muscle, not even the animals. It was as if everyone was holding their breath, waiting to hear Aunt Penny's response.

"I'm not seeing anyone," Aunt Penny finally said. "I only went out with Harrison because I didn't think you liked me. I was trying to move on."

"You were?" Mr. B said.

"Yes," Aunt Penny said. "Arthur Beiderman, I've been in love with you for years."

They looked at each other for a long moment.

Finally, Hyacinth couldn't take it anymore. "Kiss her!" Hyacinth whispered to Mr. B.

Without looking back at Hyacinth, Mr. B put his hand under Aunt Penny's chin, and he followed Hyacinth's advice.

The banquet hall erupted in cheers.

"This is the best conference I've ever been to," a woman standing at the table next to Jessie said.

# THURSDAY, AUGUST 21

# Twenty-Eight

On Thursday, the Vanderbeekers woke to a beautiful crisp morning at their campsite in San Luis Obispo. A mile down the way, Papa and Oliver were at their own campsite since Papa had had to miss their scheduled camping trip when he made his emergency visit to Elberfeld. While Oliver and Papa went fishing and hiking, everyone else swam in the lake and explored the town. Aunt Penny decided to join Mr. B, Orlando, Mama, Isa, Jessie, Hyacinth, and Laney rather than stay in her beautiful, clean hotel room. They spent the evening sitting around the campsite, Mr. B and Aunt Penny next to each other on the same log, holding hands. Isa watched them with a certain amount of smugness. She had, after all, predicted their affection for each other from the very beginning.

After a good night's sleep under the stars, Papa and Oliver rejoined the family and they had breakfast together. While they packed up the van, Orlando received a phone call.

"Hello?" Orlando said into the phone. There was a pause. Then Orlando looked at Jessie with his eyebrows raised. "Hi, Dr. Bonavita. How are you this morning?"

"Isn't that the Barkley person?" Laney asked.

"Shhh!" Jessie and Isa said.

Orlando continued to look at Jessie as he listened, then turned and walked toward the woods with the phone. Everyone watched him, but he was too far away to hear what he was saying.

"Why do you think Dr. Bonavita is calling him?" Isa asked.

"I'm going closer so I can hear," Laney said, but Jessie grabbed the back of her shirt so she couldn't move.

They stood there, watching him and wondering, for the next twenty minutes. Finally he put his phone in his pocket and returned to the campsite.

"What was that about?" Mr. B asked.

"That was Dr. Bonavita," Orlando said, looking shocked.

"We know *that*," Laney said.

"What did she say?" Jessie said.

Orlando looked at Jessie. "You shouldn't have done it."

"Done what?" asked everyone except Jessie.

"It should have been yours," Orlando said.

"What should have been yours?" Oliver asked Jessie.

"I was happy to do it," Jessie said. "And honestly? I don't think I'm a California person. It's a little *too* pretty here, if you know what I mean."

"Can someone please tell me what is going on?" Mr. B asked.

"I got the scholarship," Orlando told him.

There was an eruption of cheers and exclamations.

Once things calmed down, Isa asked, "How? You missed your interview."

"Well," Orlando said, looking at Jessie again, "apparently *someone* took her interview time to talk about *my* achievements instead of her own."

"You did?" Mama said, putting her arms around her daughter.

"It wasn't a big deal," Jessie said.

"So Dr. Bonavita called me," Orlando continued, "to see if I'm really as good as Jessie and my application and my references said I was. And since it didn't feel like a formal interview, I wasn't nervous about it at all. Then she offered me the scholarship."

There was more cheering and hugging.

"I'm so proud of you," Mr. B said. "But does that mean you're going to spend next summer at Berkeley?"

"That's the plan," Orlando said.

"That's . . . great," Mr. B said, his eyes instantly filling with tears. "But of course I'm going to miss you."

"I don't want you to go," Laney said.

"Me either," said everyone else.

"But of course, we want what's best for you," Mama said. "Even though we'll miss you terribly."

"And we love you and support you one hundred percent in whatever you want to do," Papa added.

"Really?" Orlando said. "Do you mean that?"

And truly, it was such a ridiculous question that

everyone just surrounded Orlando and hugged him from all sides as hard as they could.

❖ ❖ ❖

The Vanderbeekers, Orlando, and Mr. B ended up spending the day in San Luis Obispo, waiting for Aunt Penny to be done with her conference. They went to the beach, watched elephant seals sunning themselves on the shore, and drove along Highway 1. In the mid-afternoon when Aunt Penny was done, they drove back to the convention center. Mr. B rode in Aunt Penny's car to keep her company on the way home as they caravanned back to Monterey.

Papa, who was driving Ludwig, followed Aunt Penny's car north but saw that she didn't take the exit that led to her house. Instead, they found themselves heading back to Point Lobos. They parked and got out of the van.

"Since we didn't really get to spend time here yesterday," Aunt Penny said, "I thought we should stop by now. It's such a beautiful evening. I thought we could watch the sunset."

They took Granite Point Path, which hugged the

shoreline of Whalers Cove. There were beautiful pines behind them. They stopped to look for sea otters and harbor seals. Shorebirds swooped from the waves to the skies.

"This is the same view our great-grandfather had all those years ago," Jessie said as they looked out onto the cove.

"This was the place that had Pop-Pop thinking about the road trip to begin with," Isa said.

"I can see why our great-grandfather loved it so much," Hyacinth said. "I'm glad we could come here."

They looked out at the cove, at the ragged rocks that jutted into the Pacific Ocean, at the sea otters floating contentedly among the kelp. They had crossed the entire country for this view.

"To your great-grandfather!" Papa said, lifting his water bottle in the air. "And to Pop-Pop!"

"To Great-Grandfather and Pop-Pop!"

# FRIDAY, AUGUST 22

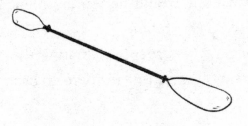

# Twenty-Nine

On Friday, they went on their sea kayaking tour, an event that convinced Hyacinth she wanted to be a marine biologist just like Aunt Penny when she grew up. While they were out in the kayaks, Hyacinth scooped up some seawater in a jar, then added shells and some sand when they got back to shore. She twisted the lid back on tight and stuck the jar in a corner of the van next to her seat.

By the time they returned to Aunt Penny's, she had gotten a call from the New York Aquarium. Apparently there had been conversations between the Monterey Bay Aquarium and the New York Aquarium about a possible research partnership, and Aunt Penny was being considered for the liaison position.

It meant that she would be visiting New York City soon!

The evening was spent celebrating the wonderful news, packing, and getting ready to go back across the country.

It was time to go home.

# SATURDAY, AUGUST 23

Miles to Home: 3,041

# Thirty

On Saturday morning, Aunt Penny helped the Vanderbeekers, Mr. B, and Orlando pack everything back into Ludwig. There was an extended, tearful goodbye to Aunt Penny, Peaches, and Cream, but finally they all got in the car and Papa pointed Ludwig eastward. Thus began the three-thousand-mile journey to the brownstone on 141st Street. It ended up taking eight days to get back home.

They faced three unexpected thunderstorms, a tornado warning, two flat tires, and a brief scare that Franz had gotten lost while they were at a campsite in Wyoming. (They found him sleeping under the van after an hourlong search through the woods.) Additionally, their attempt to return Ramona Quimby to the Harris family in Elberfeld was fruitless. Ramona had bonded to Laney and decided that she was a Vanderbeeker, and she kept on sneaking back into the van instead of rejoining the flock. Uncle Sylvester, Aunt Amelia, and Sabine graciously said that they could keep her.

When they finally made it to New York City, they could not wait to be back in their brownstone.

But first, they had to make one more stop.

Pop-Pop was buried at Woodlawn Cemetery near Van Cortlandt Park in the Bronx. The Vanderbeeker kids had never been there, but Papa knew exactly where Pop-Pop's gravestone was. It was right next to the place where Papa's mom was buried, at the northeastern corner of the property next to a large elm tree.

"Lennox Charles Vanderbeeker, 1955 to 2000. Marianna Amayah Vanderbeeker, 1957 to 1982," Jessie read out loud.

"I like their names," Hyacinth said. She had brought the jar from their kayaking trip with her, and she slowly untwisted the cap and knelt beside Pop-Pop's grave. "We went to Whalers Cove, Pop-Pop. It was beautiful."

Everyone gathered around the gravestone.

"I miss you, Dad," Papa said, touching the carved stone that spelled out his father's name. "I wish you could have been with us."

Hyacinth poured the water from the Pacific Ocean along with the sand and shells into the ground and stood up. With a smile, the Vanderbeekers, Orlando, and Mr. B headed back to Ludwig Van, ready for home at last. Three weeks wasn't very long, yet the Vanderbeekers, Orlando, and Mr. B had driven across the entire country twice, survived extreme heat and thunderstorms and a thieving raccoon, acquired a pet chicken, and found love in Monterey.

They had eight miles left of their road trip, and Hyacinth could already picture the redbrick brownstone on 141st Street: the familiar stoop with the black iron handrails that curved gracefully upward like wispy clouds, the sunlight dappling through the big oak tree with its leafy branches, the joyful spin of the weathervane on a blustery day.

The brownstone was waiting for them, and Hyacinth could not wait to be home.

# Acknowledgments

This book has been a joy to write, and I am always so grateful to embark on this journey with my fantastic editor, Ann Rider. It is an honor to work with someone who loves the Vanderbeekers as much as I do! Many thanks to the team at Clarion/HarperCollins, who have taken such care with these books. Sending love to the great Sammy Brown and Vaishali Nayak for their hard work getting this book into the hands of readers; David Hastings for the gorgeous book design; Katya Longhi for another magical cover; Jennifer Thermes for the charming map endpapers; and Mary Wilcox, John Sellers, Mary Magrisso, Alia Almeida, Mimi Rankin, Emma Meyer, all of the sales reps, and copyeditors Erika West, Colleen Fellingham, and Susan Bishansky.

I'm always so happy to work with Ginger Clark, lover of wombats and a fierce advocate for me in every way. Many thanks to Nicole Eisenbraun for her support these many years!

Librarians, teachers, and booksellers are national treasures and deserve palaces and an endless supply of delicious things to eat. I am thankful for all the ways they share their love of reading with young people.

Hugs to Amy Poehler, Kim Lessing, Matt Murray, and the entire Paper Kite team!

One of the best parts about being a writer is being surrounded by compassionate and creative colleagues in the Kid Lit community. So many writer friends have encouraged, advised, and made me laugh this year. Thank you to Sarah Mlynowski, Christina Soontornvat, Stuart Gibbs, Max Brallier, James Ponti, Hena Khan, Rebecca Stead, Jenn Bertman, Supriya Kelkar, Vicki Jamieson, Linda Sue Park, Gbemi Rhuday-Perkovich, Gayle Forman, Jarrett Lerner, Laura Shovan, Janice Nimura, and Celia C. Pérez.

Lots of love to Lauren Hart, Emily Rabin, Katie Graves-Abe, Harrigan Bowman, Kate Hennessey, the Glaser family, and the Dickinson family for being wonderful, amazing people. A special shout-out to the communities that have inspired and encouraged me, including the Town School, Book Riot, Read-Aloud Revival, the New York Society Library, the Renegades of Middle Grade, the New York Public Library, All Angels' Church, and my Harlem neighbors.

I couldn't do any of this without my family: Dan, Kaela, and Lina. They have never stopped believing in me, and I am blessed beyond measure.

# READ ALL
# THE VANDERBEEKERS'
## ADVENTURES!

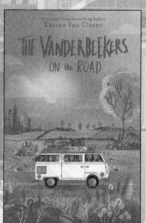

Look for a new
Vanderbeekers novel
coming in Fall 2023!